DISCARDED

891.86
L972

Lustig, Arnost
    Darkness casts no shadow

D0938472

CHILDREN OF THE HOLOCAUST
THE COLLECTED WORKS OF ARNOST LUSTIG

# DARKNESS CASTS
# NO SHADOW

DISCARDED

# DARKNESS CASTS NO SHADOW

by Arnost Lustig

TRANSLATED By
Jeanne Němcová

INSCAPE / PUBLISHERS / Washington, D.C.

COLLEGE OF THE SEQUOIAS
LIBRARY

Copyright© 1976 by Arnost Lustig

*Printed in the United States of America. All rights reserved.
No part of this book may be used or reproduced in any manner
whatsoever without written permission except in the case of
brief quotations embodied in critical articles and reviews.*
For information address INSCAPE Corporation, 1629 K Street, N.W.,
Washington, D.C. 20006

Library of Congress Catalog Card Number 76-41232
International Standard Book Number: ISBN 0-87953-406-0

Library of Congress Cataloging in Publication Data

Lustig, Arnost.
Darkness casts no shadow.

(His "Children of the Holocaust", v.2)
1.   Holocaust, Jewish (1939-1945)—Fiction.
2.   World War, 1939-1945—Children—Fiction.
I. Title.
PZ4.L97Ch vol. 2 [PG5038.L85] 891.8'6'35s
ISBN 0-87953-406-0      [891.8'6'35]      76-41232

*For My Mother*

The author would like to thank Ed Kessler, Myra Sklarew, and Henry Taylor for their valuable aid in the preparation of the manuscript. Above all, I want to thank Jeanne Němcová for her noble and elegant contribution.

# 1

*Is everything lost in the darkness?*

"He's started shooting," said the first boy, whose name was Danny.

"The crazy fool," the second replied uneasily. He looked up into the shredded clouds. "He probably thinks we're soldiers."

There had been no peace in the sky since the plane appeared. The flat car tossed from side to side and the wind lashed them, blowing soot into their eyes. The pilot had evidently decided that the train below was now in the right place. But first he'd give them a demonstration of dive-bombing techniques complete with acrobatic tricks.

"If he intends to blow up the locomotive," the first boy said, "he'll have to do it before we get to the tunnel."

It was an American plane, lumbering along above the train.

9

"And if his target isn't only the locomotive and he starts shooting up the rest of the train, there's no sense in us hanging around," the first boy said.

The second boy, whose name was Manny, swallowed an answer.

"Either that or we're goners," the first went on: "We don't have much time for arguing, Manny."

His mouth dropped as he looked up at the plane and then at his companion, then at the back of the freight car they were riding on. "Will you jump after me? Or do you want to go first?"

The pilot set his sights on the train again. Manny wanted to wait and see whether he'd realize his mistake—that the train wasn't an army transport, even though there were guards with rifles in every freight car.

The train was moving faster now through a wide ravine that ran between two steep wooded hills. It whistled, long and plaintively. The German engineer either wanted to unnerve the pilot or make him understand it was a prisoner train. On the other side of the tunnel, the hill was covered with fallen trees. A stream flowed through the meadow to the right, bubbling into white foam over the stones. The weather had been good, with showers in the morning. The sky was a bluish-grey above the scraps of clouds.

The noise of the airplane was coming from a different angle. The pilot was gaining altitude again. Now he flew at the train in two big S-shaped arcs. He was confident they couldn't get away. As the pilot headed straight toward the railroad tracks, there was a knocking noise through the roar of his motor as though he was running out of gas or as if one cylinder had failed.

"What about Frank?" asked Manny, who had a freckled face. His ears stuck out; they were very obvious because his head was shaved. His cheek bones were covered by thin bluish skin, as delicate as a girl's.

Frank was a man of about forty. He was in the left corner of the freight car close to the engine, sitting on several blankets, next to a German soldier with corporal's insignia.

Instead of answering, the first boy began to unbutton his overcoat. It reached almost to his ankles and the back was scribbled with black and white paint so everybody would recognize him if he tried to escape. They all had *KL (Konzentration Lager)* painted on their backs in white paint too.

His dirty fingers, stiff with cold, tugged at the buttons. He kept watching the plane.

He stretched out his arms to keep from falling as the train lurched on.

The older boy also began to unbutton his coat. "He could go a little faster," he said.

The second boy was watching Frank too. The plane's machine gun fired and it didn't stop. The bullets whistled past the engineer's cab and the coal tender. The passengers in the first coach must be chopped up into little pieces by now. The pilot banked, as though he wanted to slice his wings right through the middle of the train. The approaching rattle of the machine gun mingled with the noise of the engine and of the wheels racketing along the tracks.

"Don't you want to ask Frank one more time?" asked the second boy.

The locomotive rushed towards the tunnel with a loud whistle and the train bounced and clanged from side to side. The valley had a slight downhill slope. —We're in the tenth car, the first boy thought to himself. It'll be our turn when he comes round the third time. He could see the plane's underbelly, grey as a fish. The pilot's maneuvers were precise and elegant. He had plenty of time.

"I'll try once more," the first boy said.

"That guy up there can give us a great military funeral," the second said.

Frank hadn't been the same since his last birthday, the second boy thought to himself. It hadn't taken long for him to lose his spark.

The first boy wondered whether there was an anti-aircraft emplacement on the tunnel, and, if there was, whether whoever was manning it was going to let the pilot shoot up every soul on the train before bringing down the plane. Afterwards, they'd give the pilot a funeral.

The plane would look like a smoldering pile of tin. They'd already seen plenty of piles of tin along the tracks.

"We've got nice weather," said the first boy. "It's not raining, so we won't skid."

"There's a lot of wind," the other boy said.

"It's early yet."

"That's good."

On his second pass, the pilot came in from a hair-raisingly steep, banked curve and the machine gun began to bark, breaking into the regular clatter of the wheels over the seams in the tracks. The roar and whistle of the motor above them, running at top speed, came in spurts. There were bursts of vapor a few feet from the ground.

Something flickered in Manny's eyes, as though the pilot, the train, six days without eating, and the events of the last three years were shadows out of which he was about to step.

The boys' overcoats were water-soaked and reeked. The second boy had narrow shoulders. He shifted from one foot to the other, testing his legs and muscles to make sure they were still functioning, as if wondering whether he'd be able to run after they jumped out. And how far he could get. Not being able to run more than a short way was as bad as not jumping out at all. It was a waste of time, thinking about it. They'd been waiting for this chance for eight months. Before that, they'd waited two years and four months. They'd even thought about it earlier, but that was in Prague and they still didn't know what was in store for them.

"He's not going to dive," the first boy said. "Maybe just once."

Finally Frank raised his eyebrows. He always did that when he didn't know what to do next, but the boys didn't know it.

"Frank doesn't want to," the first boy said. "He's scared."

"The engineer's putting on the brakes," observed the second boy.

"Nobody can fool me anymore. OK, let him stay behind and get killed."

12

"He can't stop this train now. He ought to let off steam, or it'll kill him. I guess he wants to jump overboard too."

The plane was ahead of the locomotive again, nose to nose.

The guard, who was sitting at the back of the car beside Frank, was from somewhere in Transylvania. The boys watched him raise his gun and aim at the plane.

The hill ahead looked like a sugarloaf. Fallen pine trees lay at the bottom. There were patches of snow on the rocky northern slope.

The dark mouth of the tunnel was suddenly illuminated. It looked like a stone horseshoe against the hill. The tunnel was obviously too short to shelter more than the engine, if the engineer managed to stop in time.

The brakes caught briefly, then slipped again. The wheels screeched and sparks flew.

The two boys grabbed each other to keep from falling. The older man watched them calmly.

Looking at the tunnel, Manny was reminded of something Frank had said when they'd been in the old camp. He'd watched them building the crematorium and the gas chambers. "It's not gas, it's a tunnel and people come out on the other side," he said.

The plane began to climb again, making a whistling noise. It seemed to be tethered to the sky with an invisible cable. When it reached 500 meters, the plane bounced as if there were a hill in the clouds, and turned its nose back toward the earth, ready to finish what it had started so leisurely.

The line, marked out by gun and cannon, shortened the distance between the pilot and the boiler of the engine, wiping out the dotted line of bullets. The thing that made noises like a missing cylinder suddenly perforated the boiler in many places. Steam began to escape in hissing jets from holes the size of peas. The brakes screamed.

The fireman and the engineer jumped off the train and ran along the bank of the stream, trying to reach the tunnel.

"Now, Manny!" said the first. He tore off his coat and dropped it on the floor of the railroad car. Frank must have noticed even though he was watching the tail of the plane

13

as it passed over the end of the train. He stared at the second boy who slowly began to take off his coat.

"He'll come back and shoot this train up like a field mouse," said the first boy.

Frank was glaring at them angrily now and at the same time, pleadingly.

The engineer and the fireman melted into the shadowy stone walls of the tunnel.

"I'll go first," said the second boy. Then he jumped over the side.

As soon as the roaring plane was farther away and when the train had almost stopped, screams could be heard from the first coach, which had gotten a dose of machine gun bullets by mistake. That coach was filled with women, prisoners who had taken part in the Warsaw uprising and were caught a year ago while hiding in the sewers. It looked as though the wind was sucking the plane back into the sky.

The second boy closed his eyes when he jumped. He had no idea how long it took—maybe two or three seconds. He turned his head. He felt a few sharp jerks. The train had come to a stop. It was the fastest he had moved in six days during which he'd had nothing to eat but grass, roots and a piece of turnip Danny had grabbed out of a freight train going in the opposite direction. There was light all around him, but it was like darkness. He waited to feel the impact of the earth. He knew he mustn't fall back against the train or forward into the creek. He must know *how* to fall; he mustn't sprain anything. Or land on a rock.

He realized he didn't have the best shoes for this kind of exercise. They were no more than remnants of shoes, tied together with rags. He'd given his shoes to Danny in exchange for the piece of turnip.

He wished he could skip these next few seconds or the next hundred years. Just so he'd be somewhere else, far away from here. At that moment he hit the ground. Danny was right beside him.

"Let's go!" said Danny. "Come on, Manny!"

The first boy plunged into the creek. His knees gave way,

14

but then he pulled himself together and dashed on, a few paces ahead of the second boy. The water was ice-cold.

The plane was above them again, spilling its golden bullets in double streams of fire into the rest of the train. It was easier to run without coats.

In those first few seconds, everything was erased that had happened to them during the past three years. And the three years before that. Like the meadow they were running through, which brought them closer to the first fallen pines. The feeble early springtime sun was shining on the other side.

Seen at close hand, the hill was bell-shaped. It rose gradually at first, then got steeper.

The pilot had turned away again. The summit of the hill, when they looked up at it, was like the wall of a precipice. Woods began on the other side.

The Transylvanian had just jumped off the train, hampered by his gun.

At first, the second boy thought the guard wanted to hide behind the train, away from the plane. But then he saw that he was shooting at them.

People were jumping out of the freight car the boys had been in. And out of the others too. But not many, because the other guards had also started shooting.

The boys were halfway up the hill. —They'd have shot us anyway, the second boy thought. He looked over at the first boy as he ran. That encouraged him, but it scared him too. It never occurred to them to stop.

The pilot was firing at the train, which kept the soldiers from chasing the boys. He fired into the supply car and the caboose.

"Faster, Manny!" the first boy panted.

The other boy breathed heavily. He dropped his chin on his chest. The climb was worse than he'd expected. The bullets whizzed all around. The Transylvanian was aiming right at him. —He'll get me first, straight in the back.

Both of them had to slow their pace. Manny clawed at the earth to keep from slipping. The earth grew softer as they neared the top. Twice, the second boy had to bend

15

double before he could take another step. He tried not to slip backwards.

"Faster!" called the first boy.

The second boy lifted his head. He saw what used to be his old shoes on the feet of the boy ahead of him. In that split second, he remembered the turnip and the way it had tasted. Like the way a cow's breath smells.

He slogged through the mud up to his ankles. He told himself to run. He wasn't thinking about the Transylvanian guard and his gun anymore.

The clear sky was curtained by the hillside and nothing was left of it but a thin sliver of light.

The hillside rose toward the tree trunks, but they thinned out again near the summit. The boys leaned against the trees and then pushed on again. Some of the stumps were rotten and some logs, caught in creases of earth, rolled away when they leaned against them.

The second boy crawled on all fours. He was panting. They were a little less than three quarters of the way up the hill. He could feel a searing pain in his chest. He knew he couldn't stop it as long as he kept running, and he knew he mustn't stop. Both sides of his lungs felt torn. His heart was beating wildly.

After a few seconds, he felt the first stabbing pain in his kidneys. He knew he hadn't been hit by a bullet. He clutched at his side. He couldn't inhale or exhale anymore; all he could do was gulp for air. He tried to leave more time between inhaling and exhaling. Then he decided that of all the people who had ever mattered to him, Danny was the only one who was still alive. He tried to imagine what would happen to him if he'd lie down, catch his breath and rest until the pain loosened its grip on his body. The goal on which he fixed his sights was no longer the top of the hill and the sky, but the first boy's back. It kept getting farther and farther away as the space between them widened.

The second boy plodded on in the footsteps of the first.

As they plunged through the mud and underbrush, the bullets reminded him of the train. He was wrapped in pain,

16

the way the darkness was wrapped in light and the stones in water.

A bullet from the Transylvanian's gun whizzed between his legs. Instead of the American plane, he briefly imagined a fish swimming at great depth. It was the same color as mud and as this hill. He looked up at Danny's feet.

Fleetingly, he thought it might really be quite pleasant if the Transylvanian would shoot him. Not just in the leg or spine. Or the pilot could hit him.

For a moment the second boy paused. He tried to straighten. Quickly, he doubled over. He took a step and the pain stabbed again. He tried to walk, bent over. He felt like a clock that breaks down because somebody has wound it too tight.

His legs felt as if they were made of wood. He was no longer looking forward to running down the other side of the hill. Having the mountain between themselves and the guards' guns suddenly didn't seem so important anymore.

Step by step, they were nearing the top of the hill. The first boy turned off at an angle so the climb wouldn't be quite so steep.

The second boy pleaded with himself to hang on, to crawl the rest of the way to the top, if he had to. He pleaded with his chest, with the pain in his side, with his muscles and legs. With his eyes and with his fate.

Then he stumbled and fell and knew he couldn't get up again. He knocked a fist against his forehead. Then he simply writhed on the ground, trying to ease the pain, telling himself that keeping down made it harder for the snipers below.

"Manny!" The first boy turned.

He was crawling on his hands and knees, clutching at roots to keep from slipping.

"Manny!" he urged. "Come on . . . just a little bit more. A few steps." There was mud in his eyebrows and tears streamed from his bloodshot eyes, as though they were trying to wash away the dirt.

"Just a little further, Manny—." He looked up, then turned away. "We're almost there!"

A wind was blowing along the ridge of the hill. It made the words sound ragged.

"What's wrong with you?" asked the first.

The second boy was startled by the sound of his own voice. He lay in a muddy furrow between two stumps. He had watched Danny climb, bit by bit, until he turned and saw him lying there.

"Get up!" Danny called over his shoulder. "Get up!" And he plunged on.

# 2

The plane was just above them. The second boy rested his closed eyelids on the earth. The pilot circled the valley, the train and the hill. —Maybe he's photographing us, Manny thought. Then two rows of shells spattered alongside him like heavy rainfall in water and were swallowed by the sticky mud. More shells lashed into the earth above his head. He didn't even bother to open his eyes. The pilot probably thought the red cross on the staff coach was just another German trick.

—I couldn't care less, the boy said to himself.

The pain had eased a bit.

The pilot wasn't shooting anymore. He could still hear shooting down in the valley. The stump had protected him. They didn't know how to shoot. Bad marksmen. A lot of them who had been good marksmen weren't shooting anymore.

19

Suddenly Manny was swamped by an awful loneliness. Only occasionally did he think he could escape it, which is what he thought when he jumped off the train. It always came back. It was a loneliness which felt the way mud looks; it was the roar of the airplane overhead and the shooting down below and it was Danny's footsteps getting further away.

—Maybe Frank Bondy will live through it. I'm all by myself too, like Bondy down there. Like Danny is, somewhere up ahead. How often have I been so lonely?

In front of his eyes, Manny saw the whole thing. That crushing loneliness had come back again.

*That September afternoon in 1944, a heavy fog rolled in over the bare plains of Poland. It rolled in waves, over people's bodies and into their souls. A thin, translucent fog. Through it he could see the stumpy brick chimney above the square building where the ovens were. Flames were licking out of it, smelling of burning bones and grease, purple and russet-colored flames, which congealed into a black cloud of soot from which ashes fell like rain. Everybody wished for wind or for the earth to rotate in the opposite direction. The ashes had a bitter taste. They were strange ashes, different from those left by burnt wood or coal, old rags or paper. They contained within themselves fire or human breath, even though they were as cold and dead as each ash is. There were people who shrank away, repelled, yet they held their hands out to catch the ashes as they fell. Then they looked at them or closed their eyes.*

*A song from Strauss's Die Fledermaus kept running through his head. He and his family had gone to see it in the clandestine cabaret in Theresienstadt a few days before they were sent to Auschwitz-Birkenau. That was shortly before Father was made into soap. The purplish black smoke came later, after the roaring of the invisible ovens had ceased, and after that, there were waves of whiteness out of which fine ashes swam. That song and the fog melted together for him, spreading out over the length and breadth of the plain, a curve of melody and a web of words,*

20

*saying you'll be happy if you just forget what can't be changed.*

*He'd felt terribly alone. He couldn't understand it. He stood by a cement pillar and sang. The soldiers, the SS, the kapos and the prisoners all thought he'd gone out of his head. Everything was done to make a person feel alone; some called it maturity or being grown up and it had two sides, like a slice of bread, because when a person feels deserted and alone, he is no longer bothered by anything, so he's no bother to anybody, not even to himself. That's why no one passed up a single portion of bread, even though they probably didn't eat it with the same appetite as yesterday or as they would tomorrow. They had just come back from watching the hanging of some prisoners who had mutinied. They may have been innocent or guilty, but they had insulted the guards, so now they were swinging in the wind and the ashes, rain and snow came sifting down on them.*

*Sometimes it went so far that he felt no responsibility even for a part of his own mind or body. He was unable to tell his left hand from his right, his feet from his hands, and one hair from the other, as though they were branches of a distant tree. Yesterday's rain and tomorrow's decay.*

*He'd seen a few people who had been turned into absolute strangers to their own family.*

*That lonely feeling had come back to him at Auschwitz-Birkenau, which was as big as hundreds of military outposts, or thousands of villages put together. A planet of the night, but of different nights than he had ever known.*

*That evening, he stood close to the wire, looking at the tufts of grass and envying every blade. He envied the grass for the touch of the sun and wind. He wished he were a blade of grass, feeling whatever a blade of grass could feel.*

*Beyond the wire there was a no man's land between the men's and women's camps. He saw a herd of women, most of them naked, carrying something under their arms. Shoes, probably. You couldn't tell. Their heads were shaved. The last twenty women were wearing flimsy shirts. They were barefoot. The wind was cold. This was another planet too,*

*FRAUEN KONZENTRAZION LAGER (FKL), the women's camp, rows of barracks, but one within sight, almost in reach of his hand.*

*He couldn't shake off the idea that since all that was left of Father was that song, the purple smoke and a few ashes, it might have been better if something had happened to Mother. He prayed he wouldn't see her among those frail, naked, barefoot women, picking their way through the October mud and stones and snow. He didn't want to be like those men who wave goodbye to their mothers as they go into the gas, or those who closed their eyes so they wouldn't see their wives filing into the showers. He looked carefully. He was glad when the naked ones had almost passed and his mother wasn't among them. There were just two more left. The next to last woman was his mother.*

*He was glad she hadn't seen him. He was sorry she hadn't gone straight to the gas chamber like the other women of her age, that the doctor had sent her off among the living, even though her hair was grey. He couldn't call out to her. He wasn't sure if it would be a good idea. The relief he had begun to feel left, like an ebbing wave, like a shadow of something which had no face, no shape.*

*He felt drawn toward the high tension wires. That was the easiest way out. He could imagine what lay in store for his mother. He waited until he couldn't see her anymore, until she was swathed in fog. He tried to push away the thought of where his mother was going or where she was coming from and how long she could hold out when she got to wherever it was she was going. Sometimes the women were forced to take showers when it was below zero. Those who lived through it were assigned to work.*

*The next day, he felt almost reassured that Mother must have frozen to death before she got to wherever they were going. It was a day of rain and snow. The women's wooden barracks were too far away for him to be sure of anything. And then he'd buried his mother too with that song, even though perhaps she was still alive. He could almost put himself in the skin of those women at the FKL who, after*

22

*October 4th, had to watch their sisters and mothers being hanged because they'd helped cary out fuse cords from the Buna Werke. It was with their help that the* Sonderkomando *blew up Oven Number 4 and then let themselves be shot because nobody had joined with them. Had Mother found that younger sister there, standing under the gallows, watching her elder sister's body sway? He felt himself in the skin of both sisters and of his mother, but he didn't know anything for sure and he was afraid to know, yet at the same time, terrified of not knowing. He thought about her every second of the day and he stayed awake all night, thinking of her. It was as if something had been torn out of him. It was as if they'd torn off his legs or arms, but the gaping holes looked different than when people have no legs or arms.*

*It was a raw and melancholy sort of loneliness. It was wishing you weren't alive, feeling that the best thing in the world would be* not *to be. Feeling you're in your own way, just by being alive. "That's how it goes here," a Hungarian rabbi had said once. "You don't have to accept the idea that everyone lives and dies alone," he said. It was like a huge sinking ship, where no one cries out any longer, but each hears the same old refrain, "Every man for himself." That was before his bread ration was stolen. But even that's not fatal.*

*There were plenty of people who adjusted to it. They wanted to be ready for the moment when being alone wasn't the worst thing that could happen to them.*

Manny dug his fingers into the earth and opened his eyes. His fingers were bleeding. He wondered how long the sticky, crumbling earth would hold him.

The circle the plane was making above the hilltop reminded him of something, but he couldn't think what it was. It was one of those things he'd rather forget, but he managed to think about it, now and then. The thoughts came and went of their own free will. He was now hidden from the plane's guns by the stumps.

*He'd often thought how differently people die when they're condemned to it, but before that noon, he thought about it in another way. Secretly he had hoped that, when his time came, he'd be able to die like that blond fellow from Copenhagen.*

*He remembered the blond, blue-eyed Jew from a Danish transport who was stopped by an SS officer in front of the gate of the Little Fortress in Theresienstadt. That was where people were sent who had committed some offense against ghetto regulations. "Take off your hat, you dirty Jew!" ordered the officer. The blond fellow slapped him so hard he fell down. He even managed to hit his adjutant, who drew his pistol before the officer got to his feet again and emptied his gun into him. Then Manny watched them literally trample that blond man into the mud.*

He heard the plane screech as it circled, doing aerial acrobatics for the entertainment of everybody on the ground who was still alive. Including the two boys. —That's good, he thought to himself. The second boy's eyes were fixed on his friend's back.

Danny was struggling, helping himself with his hands. The plane's machine gun blazed a trail of bullets near him. He had about eight steps left to take—Manny had thirteen. The gap had widened.

Something darkened before his eyes. But what he saw when the darkness lifted wasn't Danny's back anymore, but his belly. He wasn't going in the opposite direction, he was coming toward him.

"Give me your hand!" he wheezed. "Hurry up!"

It was hard to hear him above the noise of the plane and its gun. The pilot was aiming his cannon at the locomotive.

"We're going to have to make a run for it or we're done for," shouted Danny. "Get going!" He gasped for breath. "Do you want me to kick you? I'll kick you! Get up! Give me your hand! Manny!"

Danny seized the boy's hot, wet and bleeding hand. There was mud between his fingers. It felt like dough. Manny felt himself being jerked to his feet. But he couldn't get up.

24

The needles that had been stabbing Manny's lungs and kidneys had changed into Danny's hand.

"Come on," said Danny. "Just thirteen steps," he went on. "We're almost there." He waited. "You don't want me to drag you the rest of the way, do you?"

Below, they heard the shattered locomotive groaning and wheezing, and, above them, the plane. Vapor rose from its cannon.

"Just a few inches more, Manny," said the first boy.

He heard many different undertones in his voice—the steely groan of a ship's propeller scraping a rocky bottom . . .

—We've made it, Manny told himself. There was a forest on the other side of the hill. From the sound, several guns were still firing together. The pilot circled toward the hills and the train in an ever-widening radius. For us, it's over. The pressure of Danny's hand suddenly relaxed. For a second, Manny was afraid they'd killed him.

# 3

They were in a small, rough clearing, covered with tree
stumps. Empty tin cans were neatly piled beside the
remnants of a campfire full of wet ashes, tree bark and dead
leaves.

Danny rolled his head away and rested it against the rim
of the campfire place. Tears streamed from his eyes. His
empty stomach turned inside out. Then he coughed and
it sounded as though he was gagging. He didn't even bother
to swallow his saliva or wipe his mouth.

The treetops tossed in the wind on the other side of the
hill. The air smelled green. Here the sky looked bigger,
pale blue as it stretched off into the distance.

Danny kept on trying to vomit. He rubbed his mouth
against the stones encircling the campfire place and tasted
the ashes, ashes mixed with wet snow.

Manny lay on his back and closed his eyes. The sky felt close enough to touch if he'd just reach out. But he didn't want to. He couldn't. There was a deep furrow between the stumps of the trees which had been chopped down and those blown down by heavy winds. It was a shallow bowl of earth and it had a bottom, sloping sides, trees, the surface of the earth and its center, rainwater and rain which had not fallen yet. His eyes watered. He inhaled the scent of the wet grass. It didn't matter that his mouth and ears and eyes and nose were full of sticky, shapeless clay. He had a bitter taste in his mouth, but it was different from the way the ashes had tasted in Poland. There was blood on his lips; it had a sweet taste. He tried not to notice how Danny was coughing and gagging. Then, briefly, he thought back to that autumn afternoon.

*The sky was overcast. In the fog, you couldn't see the ropes from which gaunt, rag-clad women's bodies swayed. You couldn't even see the eyes peering out through the cracks in the FKL barracks at the swaying bundles of rags the fog rolled in. Afterwards, it had rained for days. In the mornings and at night, it snowed. In between, there were ashes, drummed into the earth along with the rain. In the afternoon, there was fog. He could hear slow, languorous music. Like that last evening when they'd been with Father at the secret cabaret in Theresienstadt.*

*But now, looking back, it seemed almost pleasant. It proved people were right who had feared the transports without knowing why. There are things a person fears without knowing why.*

*When they'd ordered Father off the ramp and straight into the gas, Manny had felt more alone than ever. It was the 28th or 29th of September; he couldn't remember exactly.*

*There had been madness in his grief, sometimes loud, sometimes quiet as a whisper, like ashes drifting to earth. This loneliness suddenly had a face and a voice which it hadn't had before.*

*He couldn't understand why they'd killed his father, just because he wore glasses and was 52 years old.*

28

*He stood next to the concrete pillar and stared at the
flames. He wanted to inhale as much smoke as possible
into his lungs. He saw a low chimney. It was the crematorium. Red bricks. The pillar was new. On the other
side of the crematorium were the factories where mattresses
and soap were made. He was afraid they might order him
there. He kept looking that way as if the door might open
and Father step out, fair-haired and blue-eyed, looking like
the director of a bank, as the ARYAN GAZETTE once
wrote about him. The last of the fence posts looked quite
small in the distance. A song–the one they sang in the
cabaret–*Glücklich ist, wer vergisst, was schön nicht zum
endern ist. *A silly little song can outlive so many people.*

*He took a deep breath of the burned bones. He could
taste them. He held up his hands to catch the ashes. But
all he caught was rain or snow or fog.*

*"Be glad things are the way they are," said Danny. "You
know what would have been even worse for him and for
my father."*

*Danny never talked about it. Both of them knew how
much worse things could be.*

*But there was still to be added to it the violet skin on
Mother's fragile body. He could hear her voice. Like when
she used to read prayers to him when he was a little boy.
Her voice was lovelier to listen to than the prayers, and
when she prayed, Father always smiled.*

*He had never been able to figure out that smile. He was
afraid to look a woman in the face, fearful it was Mother.
Or was it because of something else?*

*The Hungarian rabbi used to tell Danny: "We're all on
our own ... alone ... nobody has anybody. Other people
only get in your way."*

Danny was still coughing; but he wasn't gagging anymore.
The ridge of the hill was covered with grass flattened
by wind and wet fog. There were tufts of earth and low
bushes. Manny inspected it, along with the white, sweat-
stained face of his friend.

Everything seemed different inside the woods. Nobody could find them now, even if any of the guards from the train came up looking for them. The boys lay side by side. There was no need yet to decide how long they could stay there, resting.

Manny looked across the stretch of grass ahead and focused on the furrow of stillness beside the deserted army campfire. When he took a breath and felt no pain, it was like the lifting of a weight which had pinned him to the ground.

He looked around. He touched the grass and stones, breathing in the silence that blanketed the forest and the silence which was in between them and the train.

"Everything's all wet," he said.

"It's soft," replied the first.

Danny finally stopped coughing. Manny touched his chest and felt how thin the skin was.

"Frank stayed behind," said Manny.

"He shouldn't have," replied the first boy. "It's his own fault."

"They all stayed."

"It'll be better down below. It isn't so windy in the woods."

Manny rubbed his ankles.

"That pilot massacred them," said Danny.

The wind pushed low clouds across the sky.

"Manny?" said the first. "It's behind us now."

Danny watched the clouds and the sky, the hill, the valley and the long stretch of forest.

"Everyone has to get out of it however he can." he said.

"I had an awful pain in my side. Both sides. That never happened before."

"It was awfully steep."

"It was a good thing it wasn't so steep at the beginning." He paused. "That was a funny plane. Close up, it looked awful small. I thought they had faster machines."

"I don't think about it anymore."

He brushed his hands through his hair, then rubbed his eyes. "I don't want the mud to cake," he explained.

30

After having run so fast and having lain in the grass so long, Manny was cold. He began to shiver and moved closer to Danny. When he touched him, his entire body began to tremble.

—I wasn't alone then, like I was back there on the hill, Manny said to himself.

*He remembered being with Danny in Auschwitz-Birkenau when he got dysentery, Danny got it too, because he'd fed him with his own spoon in order to show him that it isn't fatally infectious. They worked in the Auto-union car factory and then in DAW, Deutsche Ausrüstungwerke, a German munitions factory. They got something to eat only once in twenty-four hours—salty soup, to make them thirsty. The only water was in the washrooms where there was a big sign, "Warning: Not suitable for drinking."*

*Every morning and evening during the epidemic, the older boys from the gypsy barracks dragged Manny and Danny out to the* apelplatz *for roll-call. One thing became evident: you don't have to be the strongest, or the smartest in order to be able to help others. The Scharführer from Waffen SS led the weakest to the car which took them to the gas chamber and said, "We're all only people." And: "To err is human."*

*You could trust Danny. Except for the time he let Danny collect his soup ration while he was carrying rocks . . .*

*It's awfully easy to let somebody die.*

"I wish the past were as dead for me as it is for you," Manny said.

Danny was watching the silent dot which was the plane as it disappeared between the treetops and the hill, into the curving horizon.

"Crazy fool," he said sadly.

"He probably doesn't have enough gas or ammunition left. Those bullets looked like gold. Now he's going to fly back to some base and brag about what he did. I hope he took pictures. I'd like to see his face when they're developed and he takes a look at them."

31

He watched the plane with undisguised envy as it flew away.

"It's not important anymore. Anyway, we really had to run for it."

"I'm cold," Manny repeated.

Danny looked back to where he had first seen the dot of the plane in the sky. He put his arm around his shoulder.

"You *pipl*," he grinned.

"*Pipl*," replied Manny.

Nobody, except Frank Bondy, bothered debating about whether it was an inate affliction or an acquired inclination. It simply *was*. And there was a lot of it. *Pipls* were the comeliest little cherubs. Who knows where the name came from? Maybe it was derived from the German word for spigot or little pipe or hose. Maybe somebody just made it up. Nobody ever bothered to think about it.

*Pipl* was part of the vocabulary at Auschwitz-Birkenau, it was like saying "organize" when you mean "steal". But linguistics, Frank always said, was on the bottom rung of his ladder of interests.

"It doesn't matter anymore," the first boy said. "It's over and done with now."

The *pipls* were a caste. Often they were the smallest and weakest boys, but also the attractive ones who had the power. Most boys would have liked to become *pipls,* just as fifteen year old girls dream of becoming fashion models, or prostitutes in Paris or Istanbul or Belgrade.

Some youngsters dreamed of becoming a *pipl,* the way some grownups dreamed of belonging to the Gestapo or being a German army officer because of the advantages and status it brought. Plenty of food and clothes, a roof over their heads, and not having to be scared you'll be gassed as soon as you get too skinny.

At Auschwitz-Birkenau, the materials from which dreams were woven changed, but the dreams themselves remained unchanged. Being a pretty little Jewish child took on a new value.

Some parents even wished their children would be chosen

as somebody's *pipl*. There were hundreds of reasons, but the main ones always overlapped.

Sometimes the parents, or one of them, wished it for their child's sake; other times, it was for their own good, or so they thought.

When they used to lie so close together in the same bunk, just keeping warm, Danny was always scared somebody would get the wrong idea.

Danny was thinking how wonderful it was, all that lay ahead, and how it buried what they left behind, including those last few minutes when they'd been clawing their way up the hill.

"Hey, little Jew bastard," he said. "What are you thinking about?"

"About the girl Frank used to ask me about."

Danny wondered whether he hadn't just invented her. It wouldn't have been the first thing Manny had dreamed up.

"And about the forest," he went on, "And those weapons we helped to make. They probably killed a lot of people."

"I lost my cap," said Danny.

"Maybe Frank never really figured on coming with us at all," said the second.

He glanced at Manny and wiped the mud off his lips. The plane had been out of sight for a long time.

# 4

For several hours they had been walking over the same kind of hill as they'd crossed yesterday. They'd stopped arguing about how far the next town was. They didn't know exactly where they were. According to Frank, the train had been headed from Buchenwald to the camp at Dachau. In southern Germany, in other words. They were headed eastward. East was where the sun rose.

Talking had exhausted them. They plodded on through forests that had no end. Now and then, the pine trees stopped and fir and hemlock started.

"It isn't so damp," said the first. "Maybe it didn't rain here that much."

They were cold. Low sharp branches scratched their necks and cheeks and could have put out their eyes. For hours, they heard crows.

The first boy turned around. "You ought to walk faster, Manny."

The second boy understood. He tried to imagine sounds other than the cawing of the crows.

"We're really alone here," he said.

They hadn't been alone that morning. It was lucky they hadn't fallen into the clutches of the man in a green uniform, carrying a rifle.

"So far, so good," said the first boy. "We're doing all right."

It was another hour before they spoke again. The ground was level, but the woods were full of fallen trees, marshy places and holes. Sometimes they had to wade for several yards.

The crows were flying very high.

"We didn't get far this morning," said the second boy.

"We were lucky, though," remarked the first.

Manny looked ahead, noticing the different kinds of bark on the tree trunks.

When he heard the crows, he could never think of pleasant things. They started cawing in the middle of the night and woke the boys who got up and continued on their way.

—It's a good thing I'm not a soldier, he thought. He tried to keep the same distance behind Danny.

He wondered if he could catch some animal with his bare hands. He thought how people hunt down animals. Then he turned it and thought about how animals hunt down people. The first boy was thinking about food too, but in a different way. The crows made him hungry, but the idea of eating one turned his stomach. It wasn't just because they would have had no way to cook it. Sometime he broke off a twig, chewed on it for a while, then spat it out.

*Frank was the only one they'd told what the people in the camp in Gleiwitz in Poland had eaten after the tenth day or so. At the beginning it had only been the dead. Later, it was the sick too.*

*That was the day Frank handed over all his rations to them. He said it was a good thing to fast once a year and*

36

*that pious people know what they're talking about. But the
boys knew it was just an excuse. Frank said it wasn't hard
for him to imagine the three of them in Gleiwitz. For several
days they felt very close to those people from Gleiwitz.
Or whatever it was called.*

They came to a stream. Danny, who was in front, stumbled
and almost fell into the water.

The other boy lay down on his belly on the bank. Side
by side, the two boys washed their faces and doused their
heads. They drank deeply. The first lapped the water like
a cat, and the second scooped it into his palms. Then they
just let the water flow over them, as though they'd fallen
asleep.

The water was clean and cold, full of melted snow from
the mountains. The stones on the bottom were wreathed
with moss which made the water look green. Ribbons of
moss clung and waved from the bigger rocks, but the current
could not pull it away.

About three hours later, the boys crossed the same creek
again. It was evidently a long, meandering stream. They
drank again.

"It's easier in the daylight," said the first boy.

He waded awhile in the stream. He looked down at his
pants. They were soaking wet. —They'll cool me, he thought
to himself.

The first boy looked at the second. His freckles stood
out clearly.

Manny let Danny lead. He shielded his face with his
hands, as though he weren't only pushing aside the branches,
but trying to let in the light. Sometimes he even closed
his eyes and groped along. He was tired and yearned to
go to sleep, but he knew that as long as Danny had enough
strength to keep going, he mustn't hold him back. His pant
legs were wet up to the knees.

Suddenly he said, "Once when we were in the train and
I was standing in the middle of those who had already died,
and the wind was blowing around me and the sun was shining,
and everything seemed beautiful."

37

He looked at the first boy's back. Danny turned around. "What'd you say?"

"I said, if you brush it all off and think about yourself, things always look pretty good."

The first boy did not reply. It was always like that. Danny only answered when it was something he understood and something that had an answer. But sometimes he had the kind of expression he had now, before he turned away to look ahead.

He was tired and he felt like sitting down and going to sleep. Or lying down and sleeping. Even just lying down. He knew that as long as the first boy had strength enough to keep on going, they'd keep going and he knew that to keep going was the right thing to do. There was no point in holding him back. It was as if he was letting himself be dragged along.

He looked at the first boy's back. Danny turned around.

For a moment he thought they'd reached their goal. When his eyes were closed, he dreamed of clean suits; he imagined them waiting for a train going somewhere, where nobody would ask for a ticket or money. All you had to do was get aboard, sit down by the window and look out at the countryside.

*Sometimes Frank Bondy succeeded in doing something only a few others did–in making people envy him and his memories, even though 99 percent were fairy tales. But one percent was true. It was the one percent that mattered. "For some people, it's a house or maybe a window that's important. Or a beautiful fur coat, an armchair or antique or pretty dresses and shoes in the closet," he said. "For some, a chair's enough in front of a table with a loaf of bread on it and a bottle of wine or a bowl of fruit–a few pears and apples. And a view through the window of a snow-covered garden. My ideal was a house with a garden and a pond, to be able to sit in the kitchen and catch fish through the window. But it would be enough for something to snap in my brain, and I'd be scurrying off to the train station to buy a ticket to Monte Carlo. Some people know they'll live until spring and that's all they need to be happy. When I was feeling good, I just let the sun go down, knowing I'd see it again next morning. When I felt worse, and it didn't matter for what reason, every sunset seemed to me like the end of the world. Maybe it's true, that the world dies every day at evening and it's born again in the morning. But not always for everybody."*

*"Just remember, boys, every person in the world always lives at least two lives. In one, he plays with an open hand of cards so that everybody can see, and in the other, he's the only one who knows what he's got. I hope you know what I mean."*

*He claimed that everybody has the right to happiness, but nobody can show him where to find it or how to get it.*

*Then Frank had added: "I hope you know what I'm trying to say." But there were a lot of things he never explained. "For some people, it's a girl with white skin and a nice belly," Frank went on. "Everybody has his forbidden tree, the tree he's forgotten, and there's always a serpent. Maybe they taught you boys something else in your religion classes, but it's the same old story. Food, drink, houses, nice clothes, shoes, and a drop of good fun, a job which fits a person to a T. For some, yes, for others, no. Nobody ever has everything."*

*If Frank was telling the truth, he'd lost his money in the most gorgeous and exotic places in the world. By combining his talents and own personality with others, he multiplied his money so he was as rich as a king. He played roulette in Paris and Monte Carlo and entertained some of the loveliest leeches in the bars and nightclubs of Rome and London and Bucharest. When he talked of happiness, he smiled as though he was looking through a veil of sadness. He looked like he was 1000 years old. Or as though he only half-way believed some of the things he said. But he never said he had stopped believing in them. He described restaurants which serve things an ordinary person has never heard of. Caviar and pâté and spiced sausages were the least of those delicacies; there were many others. He used*

39

*to say there's nothing a person can't get along without,
but it's nice to try all these goodies just to see what they're
like. Frank never entirely admitted that it was all over.*

Danny turned around. He scratched himself on a branch.
He looked battered and bruised. His legs were covered with
mud and pine needles and dead leaves. Manny was right
behind him.

He wasn't thinking about Frank anymore, just that Danny
had probably been careless and that was why he was so
scratched and banged up.

"Don't you want to go a little faster?" Danny queried.

"I still feel knocked out," said Manny.

"Me too."

"It's as if somebody had pumped everything out of me."

—Maybe he's thinking about Frank Bondy too, Manny
decided. It was funny how close he felt to Danny. In the
camps, he'd met a few people who'd been like brothers.
Like Danny. He wasn't exactly stubborn. But he was very
determined. He didn't stick his nose into things that were
none of his business.

Danny stopped and leaned against a tree. He waited for
the other boy to catch up with him. "A lot of people would
give everything for a chance like this. Everything, Manny."

"Yeah," said the second. His thoughts were elsewhere.

He was careful about the slashing branches. He came
to the tree where Danny was resting.

"Why don't you look where you're going?" demanded
the first boy.

"I'm looking straight ahead."

"I thought you had your eyes closed," said the first boy.

"If anybody else escaped after us, they were probably
from Kohen's bunch," said the second boy.

"You think they made a run for it too?"

"I don't know."

"Why do you ask?"

The second boy wondered why Frank hadn't liked Kohen
and his people. According to Frank, they had grandiose
dreams and sacrificed the fate of other people without asking

40

them. People in Kohen's bunch had been talking about it for years. Especially since last winter. According to Frank, it was only a question of the frying pan or the fire.

Frank didn't like Transcarpathian Jews either. They never wanted to say "kill," believing that killing one man meant killing the whole world. After all they'd seen!

"Maybe they all got shot," said Danny. "They certainly would have called a meeting before they'd jump over the side."

"I can still hear those shots when he hit the engine boiler."

"I'm thirsty again," said Manny. His eyes were bloodshot. The cuts and scratches stung.

"We'd better get going," said the first boy. As he turned, he bumped his head on a tree branch. Manny waited. The first boy rubbed his forehead and kept right on going.

Manny followed.—We started on Friday the 13th, he thought to himself, if the calendar in Frank Bondy's memory was correct. Like that 13 on the rudder of the American plane. Those Polish Transcarpatharians, who never shaved their sideburns, thought very highly of the number.—If we make it, I'm going to have plenty of reason to believe in 13 too.

Kohen's people believed in something else. So did the Transcarpathian Jews. Danny believed in himself. He was a walking prayer, addressed to himself. Frank believed in the past. His version of it, at least, because they had no way of checking on him. They didn't even want to. Perhaps believing in something is our last chance. Or being strong enough to still remember. That can make the bad things a little better.

The woods were thicker now, the path choked with underbrush. Roots and rocks protruded through the moss and pine needles.

The sky glimmered through the trees. It was cloudy. You could hear pine cones falling and the screech of a startled bird as it flew from one branch to another. Crows, usually.

The Chassidim from Ruthenia, in the Transcarpathians, were just as persistant in their belief in a fun-loving God as were the people from Kohen's group in expelling Him

41

from their skulls and installing the Revolution in His place.

Frank watched them in amusement when they argued.

—I'm going to believe in myself too, in what's best and strongest in me and in what isn't good or strong either. When we get where we're going, I'm going to buy a number 13 in gold and wear it on a chain strong enough to hang a chair on. Manny felt drained, hardly strong enough to lift his feet.

He thought about the house in Prague where he used to live and all the houses nobody would ever return to and even if they would, there's nobody to wait for them. Doorbells nobody will ring.

Danny was six trees ahead.

Manny held one hand in front of his face and pushed back the branches with the other. He wondered what time it was. They'd started out at daybreak, about four o'clock in the morning. He'd never been so cold in the month of March.

He looked around. It would soon begin to rain.

All he could see were Danny's shoes. The leather had darkened and grown stiff.

He'd been watching Danny's shoes for almost an hour. It still hadn't begun to rain.

An hour later, he realised what it was about Danny's shoes that bothered him. In the train, it hadn't seemed like such a bad deal, trading a pair of shoes for a piece of turnip. Maybe Danny hadn't been so hungry.

The first boy turned. "Don't lag, Manny," he said.

He had been keeping the same speed. He wondered when it would start raining. He thought about Frank. *That winter they'd been talking about what the chances were for escaping. "Boys," he'd said, "when you turn hope into a tower so high you lose your perspective, you can't help but fall."* Sometimes he treated hope of escape like a ragdoll, tearing it apart at the seams, spilling out its sawdust or rag guts, turning it into hopelessness.

Manny's stomach growled. That was nothing new.—If I don't get cramps, I'll be all right, he said to himself. *There was the German officer in Auschwitz-Birkenau who talked*

*of the advantages of regular meals. A good number of people
lost their stomach ulcers in camp. Along with a lot of other
things. Sometimes the officer would order them to kneel
in front of a trough, pour in highly-salted fish soup and
tell them to lap it up. No spoon. He expected people to
eat like dogs.*

*The officer had never regretted the time it took him to
explain to the prisoners that they'd been born inferior and
that was why they weren't given spoons, how they ought
to be glad to lap up their soup from chamber pots. He
had a medal from the winter battle in the East, 1941/42,
the "WINTERSCHLACHT IM OSTEN," the so-called
"Frozen Meat Order."*

He wondered whether, in a way, that officer hadn't been
right.

He went back to thinking about Manya Cernovska.
Danny's lucky. He doesn't think of anything. Except maybe
that they were on their way. It made the time pass more
pleasantly.

The second boy had a fever. He knew it without even
touching his skin.

*Maybe Frank Bondy needed to have them listen to him
talk. Maybe it provided some continuity between the world
he used to live in and the world the two boys knew. It was
nice to hear Frank Bondy explain that a gentleman always
flushes the toilet when he's visiting and even at home. Or
what kind of socks a well-bred man should wear with a
plain blue necktie.*

*Frank could go on for hours, telling how he'd drunk
absinthe in Paris. It doesn't taste good, Frank said, but
it builds bridges and transforms your life.*

*The Transcarpathians whiled away time by telling how,
the tougher things got, the more joy their rabbis knew how
to extract. They knew thousands of anecdotes.*

*It was boring to hear them pray, and they prayed a lot.
Some believed the important thing wasn't who or what you
pray to or for, but just the fact of praying. Frank denied
that.*

43

*There was compassion and understanding in his eyes,
but he didn't like Polish Jews and Hungarian Jews and
he couldn't stand German Jews. Now and then he'd accept
French or Italian or Danish Jews. He'd worked out a scale
and he himself was always right at the top.*

*Frank said that some German Jews, somewhere, in the
depths of their souls, are proud of German victories and
will mourn German defeats, as if both were not the first
things that buried them. It was as if they had two souls.
The first regretted their not being German and the second
condemned their not being German.*

*"The whores on the street were three times as smart
as they were," said Frank Bondy.*

*He was a bit like the Germans too, because he never
told the whole truth. But as far as this escape was concerned,
he'd disappointed them many times. After eight months,
a few transparent lies emerged from Frank Bondy's maxims.*

*He had a fiancee in Prague whose address he'd given
to Danny. This was one of his maxims: "Truth is the best
lie." And: "You must not tell a lie, but you're not bound
to tell the truth either." Or, "You can blow up a dream
to be bigger than the night." Last time he said: "Haste
is good only for catching fleas, boys." The girl's address
was right. But he hadn't come with them.*

Manny decided it wasn't really so hard to thumb their
noses at Frank. They'd had to do it to a lot of people.
—It's not so hard to thumb your nose. Sometimes you
remember it later, but not usually. — Eat, he said to himself.
Everything boiled down to food.

They watched the crows in the treetops, cawing and honk-
ing and flapping their wings. He tried to get his mind off
the noise the birds made by thinking about the number 13.
— Eat, eat, he told himself, as though it could bring food
closer; eat, eat, eat.

Spruce and fir branches hung low. The light changed
among the upper branches where it was green and bluish.
The crows looked very black against the dark grey sky and
the clouds were like waterfalls or castles or ships tossing
in a rough sea.

44

The second boy looked down again, focusing on Danny's shoes.

"Manny," said the first.

"I'm hungry," said the second.

"Don't lose patience, Manny."

"Can you hear those lousy birds, Danny?"

He remembered sitting in the middle of the woods as a child, eating bread and butter and roasted peanuts.

"Heather's pretty, but as a kid, I was afraid of it."

His fevered eyes slipped over the back of the boy stumbling in front of him.

The first boy cast a bloodshot glance at Manny's eyes.

Suddenly something stabbed into his heel.

His knees gave way, then slowly he straightened.

# 5

By noon they were both too exhausted to talk anymore. Not even the wind refreshed them. Now and then it stopped, the humming ceased in the treetops and the silence was so complete, it drowned out the crows.

It was raining somewhere. There was a drawn-out dark sound in the air as the rain drew nearer.

"It turns my stomach, the way those birds caw," the second boy said. "Do you suppose they're following us?"

"They're always in the woods," replied the first. "They're harmless."

Manny saw how badly the first limped and Danny knew he'd noticed. He put most of his weight on his right foot to ease the pressure on the left.

"Is it bad?" asked the second.

"Why are you afraid of heather?"

"It makes me sad. I don't know why."

"Heather's beautiful."

"Does your foot hurt bad?"

"Not really," replied the other.

"Do you want me to go first?"

"It doesn't matter."

"Do you want to stop for a while? Do we have to keep going uphill? We've been walking uphill for two hours."

"We're going the right way," replied the first.

"You're just wearing yourself out."

"Don't you think it's too much uphill, Danny?"

"It's going to rain."

"Let it rain," the second boy said. "Don't be so sure I can still make it, Danny. If there's one thing about those crows that bothers me, aside from the awful racket they make, it's that they're always too high to kick. I kicked one once when I was wearing those shoes you have on now, Danny. That bird's not flying anymore."

They walked side by side. The second boy didn't need to raise his voice anymore. Maybe the first would have liked to ask where Manny had kicked the crow, but the pain in his foot was sharper now.

"Snow is sometimes beautiful, too," said the first. "When it's white. Heather and snow.

"Yeah," said the other.

"I'm not slowing down because of you."

—It's probably a nail, he decided. He could feel it. He should have known. It had worked its way out slowly, but now it was jabbing into his heel.

The wind tossed the branches and the air was full of cawing crows. Maybe Manny was right; those birds might call attention to them.

"Probably nobody pays attention to crows," he said. "Forget them, can't you, for God's sake?"

Danny stopped and leaned back against the tree, feeling like Bondy, relaxing outside a hacienda in Latin America, one foot crossed casually over the other, arms folded and head tilted back, watching the sun set over the Pacific Ocean. Or the Atlantic?

48

The second boy leaned against another tree.

The first boy wondered whether he shouldn't try to hammer out the nail with a stone. He looked around in the moss. He knew that if the pain got worse, it would slow them down more than Manny's lingering. He grinned wearily.

The second boy grinned too. He didn't want to be the first to sit down.

The second boy was chewing pine needles. He did it on and off. They had a bitter taste and you couldn't swallow them, but they were all right to chew for a while. He tried a pine cone. One kind had seeds inside and you could eat them.

"You're like a squirrel," the first boy said.

"We could make a good meal out of one of these," the second boy said.

The first boy was silent.

"Of course, it'd be lowering our standards," said the second. He paused. "I'd slow down, if I were you, Danny."

"Shut up, Manny."

The second stared at the moss. — You'd have to swallow a lot of worms if you'd try to eat a piece of moss, he thought to himself. He knew the other boy couldn't stand the idea of eating anything raw. Not just because of what they said about those people who'd been in Gleiwitz. In camp, they'd tried it with a cat. He wondered about squirrels. But it was just a thought. —A squirrel's too quick to get caught. Except a dead squirrel. There are other creatures in the forest that eat dead squirrels, though.

—Until a person goes a little crazy, like in Gleiwitz, the thought's repulsive, he said to himself. A fever is just one step from the madness, he thought, but it's still repulsive.

"We're still picky about what we eat, aren't we?"

The first boy pushed off from the tree and started walking. It went all right. He didn't want Manny to sit down. That would mean the end of today's hike. He didn't want to hear any more about all the things that can be eaten raw, either.

49

Manny tramped on after the first boy, listening to the crows as they flapped away or settled back in the treetops with the drawling, ambiguous "kraaa."

—That foot must be giving Danny a lot of pain, the second boy thought. The first boy was thinking how unfair it was that crows can fly wherever they want to and that they always have enough to eat.

"We're taking a step and a quarter for every meter," the first boy said. "We're doing fine. I can feel it in my bones, Manny. We're making good time."

The other boy was silent.

*For almost an hour, Manny had been thinking about a man in Theresienstadt who had caught and eaten crows. He was a basket-maker whom the major had kept around until, out of spite and envy, the other SS men had sent him off to Auschwitz-Birkenau in the major's absence. Everybody with a W was shot immediately on his arrival at the final station. That man believed that crows had a peculiar strength because they lived 150 years, feeding on the finest prey in the fields and forests.*

It was already late in afternoon. He wondered why Danny didn't want to take off his left shoe.

"We've left the rain behind. According to that, we can figure out how far we've come already." Danny remarked.

"I wish you could calculate it forwards instead of backwards, Danny."

"Once we get there, it won't matter."

"Have you any idea at all where we *are*? I hope we'll know by evening, Manny."

"This is still better than being shot at or gassed, isn't it, Manny?"

It sounded as though he was afraid the second boy wouldn't be able to keep up the pace.

"Does it hurt?" Manny looked down at the first boy's foot.

"You already asked me once, Manny. It hurt before, didn't it? Don't worry about it. I won't either."

The second eyed him quizzically.

The first boy stopped again and leaned against a tree. A globule of sap trickled onto his forehead from an upper branch.

The nail in his shoe made a difference.

"If I were you, I'd be careful," the second boy said.

"What for? I'm like an animal."

"Of the nail. Or whatever it is."

"You know what it is?"

"I can imagine. I'm not blind, Danny. If it's a nail, you could develop blood poisoning."

"I'll get there even with blood poisoning."

"Like hell you'll get there with blood poisoning!"

"I don't know what's inside the shoe," the first boy said.

"Well, have a look, Danny. Look, while it's still light."

"I don't need light for that."

"How far do you suppose we've come today?"

"We got a pretty late start."

"It was four o'clock in the morning."

"It's hard to judge distances. And there's no other way we can go except through the woods."

"Frank probably knew why he stayed behind."

"There's no use getting mad at him."

"I'm not pouring out my anger; I'm tired, Danny."

"He's just a son of a bitch, Manny, he's no prophet."

"Yeah."

"When somebody's a bastard, I don't care if he croaks."

"Every bastard *ought* to croak so they don't make things difficult for people who aren't bastards."

"Maybe he knew."

"Frank would never have made it this far. He hasn't got it in him. That's why he stayed behind, Manny."

The first boy's voice sounded tired and heavy.

The second boy spoke feverishly. "Don't you really want to sit down for a second, Danny?"

"Frank wouldn't have been able to keep going long without food, Manny. He wouldn't have been able to get through

51

COLLEGE OF THE SEQUOIAS
LIBRARY

that swamp and underbrush. He couldn't have stood the cold at night. He'd have been eaten up by fever and exhaustion. He couldn't cover this distance, always keeping on the move like you and me."

"Maybe they sent back a new engine and a hospital coach so the rest of them could go on to wherever it was they're going. Maybe they'll be able to escape in a better place, closer to the border."

"I wouldn't believe Frank now, even if he told me what time it was, Manny."

"What if that Transylvanian tipped him off and they came to an agreement or something? Frank could have convinced him that he'd help hide him after the war."

"More than likely they shot them all. And even if they sent a new locomotive and took them somewhere else, all they'd do would be to shoot them."

He paused. "Manny, have you got a fever?"

"Frank couldn't stand not eating or sleeping. He couldn't take it, freezing cold and keeping on the go, without a rest, could he?"

"I didn't hear such a lot of shooting. Except at us."

"There was that hill in between."

"That sure was a bitch of a hill," affirmed the second.

"They wouldn't have starved those prisoners till they went crazy, Manny," the first said. "Look at what they did with us. They probably shot the rest as soon as we jumped out and made for the woods," the first boy continued. "So they wouldn't follow our example." After a moment's thought he added, "If not, then Frank certainly managed to trade his watch for something to eat."

"For what?"

"Something for *himself*. I bet you anything they shot the rest of them. Germans are scared of other people more than of anything else. Getting sick comes second. They're mostly scared of people they've done something to. They can't stand the idea of witnesses. They're afraid of infection too. They wouldn't want those prisoners on their necks, hungry and wild-eyed."

52

"If they want to keep that track open, Danny, they've surely sent for another locomotive and a repair crew."

"Maybe they don't have that many locomotives. And the sky's full of Americans."

"I guess you wouldn't make very good soap."

"You wouldn't either!"

"So far, they've had enough of what it takes to exterminate almost all of us."

"They used to, Manny. Things are different now. You and I know that."

They walked along, the first boy still in front, putting his weight on his toes, and he didn't object when the second boy caught up with him. Danny limped badly.

"You can always tell which way is north, depending on which side of a tree trunk the moss grows. The woods are thick here and we're well hidden."

"I'm almost ready to call it quits for today, Manny."

"Prague is to the east. I just wish I knew how *far* east. We discussed three possible border crossings with Frank. I talked about it once with the people from Kohen's group too. After that, it'll be easy."

"I don't care what Frank said. It's about 150 kilometers, I figure.

"How far is that, in comparison to what we've done already?"

"About three days and into the night, I guess. At this pace, we're covering about twenty kilometers or a little bit less in one day and night. But not much more. We don't have any timetable, Manny. Most of it's hills and woods, and that's always confusing. Even when we go downhill, the land around us slopes upwards. That means we're coming to a pass, but it's still pretty far. After that, it's all downhill."

"Yeah," the second said. "All I know, Danny, is that today you promised we'd be back in civilization."

"Tomorrow, Manny. You can depend on it. We're heading the right way." After awhile, he went on.

"We'll find something to eat this evening, Manny. Or tomorrow."

53

"Where, if we stick to the woods?"

Danny changed the subject. "Something must have happened back there. I'm glad we weren't there. It must have been nasty."

Both of them knew that it wasn't just the fate of people on the train that troubled them. But the farther they went, the more their thoughts were drawn back to the train. They had known how to behave then and what to do. It was something that *existed,* not something which was yet to come, which they must cope with.

"Do you really think they shot them?" the second boy asked.

"They've got peace and quiet now, that's all I know, but I'm not saying what *kind* of peace and quiet," replied the first.

"I hope that pilot made a hole in the skull of that guy from Transylvania."

"It's a wonder he didn't hit us."

"You know that Transylvanian bastard claimed he had a mother? He used to talk to me like I was already dead. For hours, he told me in his stupid German that if anybody would take the trouble of making a chemical analysis of me, I'd hardly be worth two and a half Deutschmarks. Even if I'd live to be 19. That greedy pig had it all figured out, even in Czech crowns. As a corpse, I'd be worth 25 crowns. He knew it in Swiss francs, American dollars and English pounds. Money was all he had on his mind. He enlisted in the army because he wanted money and he knew how to calculate. According to him, the greater part of your body and mine is water. That's useful in making soap. There's enough iron in us to make one nail."

"There's probably not enough in him to make even the trigger of a gun," the first boy said. That word, "nail" stuck in his mind.

"I don't have enough lime in me to whitewash the ceiling of a German outhouse," said the second. "Or enough sulphur to gas a kitten or a squirrel. You could make 24 matches from the phosphorous in me. But three and a half kilos of soap just from grease and water."

"That's why they made soap out of my dad, because they wanted to make a profit," Manny went on. "They liked his overcoat, too. His watch and his wedding ring and necktie. They wanted his underpants too, and his socks and clean handkerchiefs. So they made soap out of him and they got our apartment in Prague with all the furniture and stuff and Dad's Italian mandolin, his fur-lined gloves and 3,000 crowns he'd saved over twenty years for a rainy day."

"You've got a fever, Manny."

"Aw, forget it, Danny."

"Honest, you look flushed."

"I told you, forget it. And carbon, Danny . . . that Transylvanian figured out how many pencil fillers I'd make. They made lamp shades out of Milanek Oppenheimer and Zdenek Pick because they had such nice, delicate, young skin. That guard probably never went to school back in Rumania. He didn't really know how to shoot, either. All he could do was load a gun and pull the trigger. We were lucky that it was their dumbest, meanest soldiers who came with us. Don't think they didn't *want* to hit us. How is it possible that so many dumb hicks got as far as they did?"

—Manny must be running a very high fever, the first boy figured. What would happen to them, to him and Manny? His eyes glistened under an opaque film, and although it was cool in the forest, sweat beaded his forehead.

"Old Transylvania wasn't ashamed of washing his face with soap made out of little Jewish girls. The German warehouses are full of it. Twenty years' supply of soap. If people could drink blood like wine, Danny, they'd fill barrels and bottles with it and export it all over Europe and to the rest of the world, wherever any Germans live."

He almost whispered it.

"Listen, quit pretending you don't have a fever when you do. There's no sense fooling each other. We'll rest awhile before we go on, or if you'd rather, we can call it a day already. Or do you want to keep going till it gets dark, Manny?"

"They'd export your blood and mine like wine as far

as Australia and New Zealand. Or North America.''

"It's all the same to me if it goes to Tierra del Fuego, Manny. As long as I'm here in these woods, nobody's going to export my blood anywhere.''

"They don't give a damn for our blood in Tierra del Fuego, Danny. The only ones who give a damn are you and me.'' He spoke quietly.

"If I'd known three or five years ago what I know now, I'd have taken an axe and cracked the skull of the first German who stuck his nose in our door,'' said the second. "They taught me a lesson,'' he whispered.

The wind blew into their faces.

"I'm scared, Manny, because they're done for now,'' said the first. "They'll kill anyone who can't escape or defend himself. They won't even have time to make them into soap.''

The first boy took one step forward and then his knees gave way. He clutched at a tree.

The second boy swallowed his question. He was just about to ask how his little sister could have defended herself or escaped. Or whether Danny was putting Frank Bondy and little girls like his sister into the same category.

"Do you want to wear my cap for a while, Danny?'' he asked. He glanced down at his shoes.

*He was remembering Leonard. He could already piece together what had happened.*

*Leonard was Mother's younger brother, born in 1900. Karel, her older brother, had been stoned to death in Moravska Trebova, by the Nazis right after they moved into the Sudetenland. Because he owned a carpentry shop with a lathe.*

*Leonard was a sinewy machine operator and a bachelor, after having been engaged for a long time to a Miss Gusta Glossova, who later gave her favors to the Germans after stealing Leonard's belongings, his watch and ring. That was before it was legal to steal.*

*In Birkenau, Leonard was saved by his raven-black hair, his tall, strong body and by the fact that he knew how to*

56

*work. He had the swarthy skin of a North African Jew, a prominent Jewish nose and he could have easily passed for being 15 years younger.*

*When Manny found Leonard in Auschwitz-Birkenau, his swarthy skin was wrinkled and his eyes were as sad as if he were already dead. His hands were like big shovels.*

*Once, during a blizzard which paralyzed the whole area, the foremen ordered the lights over the machines to be extinguished to save electric power. Leonard operated two lathes that made grenade heads. The blades were dull and needed changing. He lost a lot of time, honing the blades, so he had to hurry. He was careless and that was how he got the splinter of steel in his finger.*

*He sucked at it. The blood was mixed with machine oil. By evening, he'd forgotten about it.*

*Uncle Leonard had never been one of Manny's favorite relatives. When he'd lived with them, he locked up his belongings and Manny's father never liked to see anybody locking things in his home. Tools were something Leonard was particularly careful about. He never left them lying around and didn't like to lend them.*

*Once, when Manny and his little sister had wished him a happy birthday, Leonard gave a silver five crown piece to the sister because Manny had been naughty. He promised he'd get one too when he learned how to behave.*

*But when they met in Birkenau, Leonard said blood is thicker than water, that they should stick together.*

*Three days later, Leonard's finger began to bother him. Within ten days, his whole right arm was infected and he was taken to the infirmary.*

*His hand festered so fast, you could see it happen. The medical student-aide said it was gangrene, and gave him a corner bed, but not much hope.*

*"When it turns black that way, you're at the end of your rope. Unless you let me amputate that arm of yours."*

*Leonard was in no position to know that the young man had never done an amputation before. Actually, he had, but never successfully.*

*The medic asked Leonard where he'd gotten his fine shoes.*

57

*He was a handsome Polish youth with a pleasant little face that looked like it was made out of cottage cheese. He amputated whenever he had a chance. He was obsessed with knives. He cut off fingers, arms and legs at every opportunity—and there were many. He cured everything with a file and a scalpel. He drank the alcohol he got from the German doctors, so he was usually drunk.*

*Leonard was left to lie in bed for several days until it was obvious what the Polish medic was after. Leonard's arm grew black from the fingertips up into the armpit. Then the medic knew the shoes were his.*

*The bandaged thing lying alongside Leonard was no longer his own hand. It stank so badly that Manny could hardly stand it when he visited his uncle's bedside. A boy from Ruthenia lay in the next bed and the medic used to squeeze ounces of pus from his wounds every three hours, telling him he looked just like Jesus Christ. He would examine his hands as if he wanted to nail him on the wall of the infirmary like a symbol.*

*The Ruthenian boy couldn't stand the smell of Leonard's arm either, so he had to vomit over the other side of his bed.*

*The medic hated to bandage Leonard's rotting arm, so he didn't even bother. But Leonard didn't die. He fought with that blackened scrap of meat and bone as if he were really fighting with something else.*

*That was when the little blond Pole stopped giving Leonard his food rations. He'd already stopped giving them to the Ruthenian boy. So Leonard sent for Manny. He and Danny brought the old man some potato salad.*

*"Take my shoes," said Uncle Leonard. His voice sounded different than when he'd refused to give him the silver coin, years ago.*

*"What would I do with your shoes?" said Manny. "I don't need two pairs of shoes."*

*"I'm not even going to need one pair."*

*"Didn't you hear the latest news? The war isn't supposed to last more than three months."*

"Three months? Well, maybe. For you, it's morning. For me, it's midnight."

"Don't exaggerate." Manny tried not to breathe.

The boy from Ruthenia had died. Manny didn't want to look at him, so he had to look at Leonard. He didn't want to look too hungrily at his shoes, either. They were certainly good shoes.

"What'll you wear when you get up out of bed?" he asked his uncle. "You'll be feeling better when springtime comes." He swallowed hard. "They switched on the loudspeaker in the factory today. There's going to be a thaw. When they talk about the weather, they never tell lies."

"Springtime . . . " murmured Leonard. It cost him an effort to speak.

"If you don't take the shoes, that sonofabitch is going to take them," Leonard went on. "You know, he hasn't given me anything to eat for three days?"

Manny knew that taking Leonard's shoes was like taking away the last pinch of life that was left in him. He didn't want to let him die before his last shadow of hope would flicker out.

"I could have died this morning," Leonard whispered. "I didn't do it because I wanted you to come for the shoes."

"Aw, come on," said Manny. "I'll make sure they give you your food." The smell was turning his stomach, so he got up and went out to look for the blond medical student-amputator. He left the shoes standing next to Leonard's bed.

He found him going out the door, taking some food over to the women's camp. Manny told him what he thought of him and ordered him he give Leonard everything he had coming to him and said if he didn't do it, Manny wouldn't be responsible for the consequences.

The medic-amputator looked frail. Instead of answering, the little whey-face drove his fist, carnelian ring and all, into Manny's eye and knocked him down.

Leonard had told someone: "Life is a river. A river with electric current."

59

*Before the twelve hour shifts changed, somebody dragged the old man out of the infirmary to the wire fence. Leonard had asked for this. He succeeded on the third try, when it began to rain. It was enough to extinguish his almond eyes and the gangrene, too.*

*Those infirmary patients who could walk, came to tell Manny what had happened. They told him too that the Polish medic was wearing Leonard's shoes. That night, Manny killed a man for the first time, even though he did it only in his mind. He killed him a hundred times that night. That was when he realized that a man is either born to kill or let himself be killed. That was when he stopped living in the dream that the things which were happening were an exception.*

*He waited for daybreak. He lay on the roof with a stone in his hand and waited for the medical student to appear, for the door to creak. It was raining. He could almost hear the crunch of the young man's skull. He'd done it in his mind a thousand times.*

*But in the end, he didn't do it alone. It was raining and they dragged the young Polish medic out into the rain. They didn't tell him what they were going to do. They took off his shoes and clothes and then threw him against the wire fence. He bounced back as if it were a net, so they had to push him back three times. He could have screamed, but he didn't. He simply kept mumbling his name. His chin clamped down on the wires which he clutched with his delicate hands.*

*The medical student died in the same place as Uncle Leonard had several hours before. They let him lie there. It looked like suicide. They collected his things and gave Leonard's shoes to Manny.*

*It was like a funeral for Uncle Leonard—the carrying out of vengeance and the execution of Leonard's last wish.*

"Are you sure you don't want my cap?" Manny repeated.

"Forget it, Manny . . . "

"My belly's swollen."

"Ahh . . . "

"It feels heavy, like I've got a load of stones inside."

It began to rain, gently at first, and they soon got used to it. The first boy found a stick to lean on as he walked. They went on through the rain, side by side, for almost an hour. They stopped when it came down so hard, they could barely see, and stood under a tall pine tree with a thick trunk, a dense crown and patches of moss around the roots. It protected them for a while, but then the wind shifted, and the rain came in at a slant. Afterwards, the wind turned again, but the branches still dripped.

They faced into the tree trunk. The water washed their faces and felt refreshing, running through their hair and over their necks and backs and bellies, inside their pant legs and into their shoes. It rinsed the wound on Danny's heel.

It felt as if somebody had turned a hose on them. They pressed closer to the tree trunk. The second boy covered his face with his hands and the other bowed his head until his chin touched the top of his chest.

The second boy took off his cap, because it didn't do any good. They were soaked to the skin. Defiantly, Manny turned his face into the rain. The first boy stood on one leg to relieve the pain, resting his knee against the tree trunk.

The second knelt, his forehead pressed to the bark. His neck glistened with water and his ragged clothing stuck to his body.

Finally the first boy slipped to his knees too and, for awhile, he seemed to fall asleep. But it was raining too hard, pounding against the branches and into the earth, making a strange sound, as though this was a different world than the one they knew, part of some strange life where there was neither happiness nor unhappiness. A world without sun.

The rain came down heavier and heavier, lashing at them. Sometimes Manny opened his mouth like a fish, gulping air between the raindrops. Then he pressed his hands against his face and huddled against the tree again. The first boy clutched at the tree trunk as though he were embracing it.

Neither spoke. All you could hear was rain. It rained

for almost two hours. Suddenly it stopped and the clouds began to shred apart. The sun came out. The sun lit up the forest. Its rays touched the tops of the fir trees and the branches of the bushes; they clung to the leaves and moss and old stumps. Everything looked different. A golden light lay over the shades of green, on the pine needles and stones, on the grass and tree bark, on the protruding roots, a light like crystals and bubbles. The pine needles and twigs swam in channels between the stones. Everything had changed. High in the sky, a rainbow reached like a bridge between a thousand islands of trees.

"I feel like fighting," said the second boy.

"I feel like drowning," answered the first.

"I wish Frank was here."

The birds began to sing. The sun didn't give off much warmth yet, but the water streamed down the tree trunks, finding channels, floating off the fallen twigs and leaves, flowing along the roots around the fallen log, soaking into the moss and earth.

"Yeah," said the first boy.

The air was steamy. Mist formed in the treetops too and the rainbow faded. Now and then, a breeze ruffled the crowns of the trees, setting off brief rainshowers below. The branches and bark glistened like snakeskin.

"It's early in the afternoon," said the second.

The first opened his lips but didn't speak. —Maybe he's talking to the water, thought the second.

The woods surrounded them with something that couldn't be disturbed. The first boy scanned the sky.

"Do you think we'll be dry by evening?" asked the second. "Don't you want to wring your clothes out?"

The first boy slowly began to take off his wet clothes. His naked body was so skinny, his bones stuck out. He took off his shoes and unwound the rags he wore on his feet.

Suddenly the foamy silence of the forest was full of cawing crows and when the wind stopped for awhile, you could hear the silence. The two boys were alone in the woods.

# 6

Towards evening they found a clearing with tall, thick grass, not far from where the rain had overtaken them. The crows seemed to be following them. They could hear them in the branches overhead, but they couldn't see them.

The first boy acted as if there was really nothing the matter with his foot. Manny figured he didn't want to look at it until they got to wherever they were going. He felt like water boiling away. It wasn't much different from what the Transylvanian guard had predicted.

It was a small clearing, shielded on all sides by trees and low bushes. At the edges lay uprooted pines and about a dozen stumps, overgrown with moss and toadstools. New saplings had sprouted between the roots and stalks of wild-flowers, long since wilted.

At first, the sun set slowly but then it sank fast, the way the rain had started and ended. The moon appeared in the darkening sky. But for a moment the night did not fall.

A dilapidated feeding shed stood in the grass at the other side of the clearing, opposite the stumps. Manny wondered what kind of animals came to feed here.

"Here," said the first boy.

"We can sleep over there." The second boy pointed to the shed. He sat down beside it and tried to extract some seeds from pinecones he found in the manger. They'd probably been put there for squirrels. But the squirrels had gotten there ahead of him, so all he got was a mouthful of pine needles which he couldn't manage to spit out.

The first boy sat down on the other side of the shed. He took off his right shoe first. He felt the other boy watching him. He ran his fingers through his toes, slowly removing all the pine needles and sand and mud. He groaned softly.

—This is what he was scared of, thought Manny, lying with his head on a tuft of moss.

The first boy squinted into the shoe. It wasn't a very big tack. Actually, a lot smaller than he'd thought. He could hardly feel it with his thumb.

"Son of a bitch," he said.

"How big is it?"

"Too short to hammer out."

Manny said nothing.

"My foot's going to be infected by morning," Danny went on.

"So hammer it out!"

"Why didn't *you* do it?"

"You think I'd walk on a nail? Or maybe you think I knew it was there?"

"I've lived through everything else so far, so I'll live through a tack, no?"

Danny stretched out too. For an hour, they were silent. Manny kept thinking that the first boy was probably convinced that he'd known there was a tack in there when he'd given him the shoes. Maybe it had been there, but Manny didn't know about it. It had probably worked its way out while they walked. After all, Danny was taller and heavier than he was.

64

—Maybe these shoes were good once, but they've brought bad luck to a lot of people since then, he said to himself.

"Remember how Frank Bondy used to say, 'Boys, you're still young, you believe what people tell you'?"

"It's almost better if you remember only what your Mama told you, Danny."

"She said, 'Eat shit, drink water and you'll grow up to be a rich boy'."

"I can't believe that anymore either."

The stars shone until midnight and then they disappeared. It was cold. They couldn't sleep. In the night, the trees looked like ghosts.

"Aren't you asleep?" asked the second boy.

"I'll hammer it out in the morning," said the first boy.

"Come closer."

"I'm cold too."

"Can't you lie or sit closer to me?"

"I'll scrounge us up something to eat tomorrow," the first boy promised.

"I feel like I'm in a dream," said Manny. "I *am* and at the same time, I'm not. Or as if I'm somebody else."

"You're running a fever, that's it."

"I am still awful cold."

"We're like two foxes. You look like a little fox, all curled up."

"It's as though I'm just visiting myself. It's funny. As if half of everything has nothing to do with me."

"Aw, shut up."

"I can see so many things and all there is, are these trees here, Danny—places, people, things that happened. Things I thought I forgot about. Things I thought I didn't even notice."

"What things?"

"The kitchen at home, Danny. Freshly laundered shirts my mother put away in the cupboard so I could help myself whenever I wanted to. An evening in December when she made biscuits. It smelled so good, all through the house. Biscuits and a cup of milk, Danny."

"It makes my stomach ache, Manny."

"... Thousands of beautiful things and people, but they always boil down to a few—biscuits, a cup of milk, clean shirts... "

Danny moved closer. "It's always spooky in the woods at night."

He leaned back against the shed. If it began to rain, the roof wouldn't give much protection. The moon had shifted, covered by scraps of cloud.

"It's a good thing it isn't raining," said the first boy. "The east ought to be over in that direction."

"Yeah."

"In the morning, I'll find us something to eat."

"OK."

"Now we've got to concentrate on food." He paused. "Do you still have those visions of places and people, Manny?"

"Yeah."

"Maybe we can make fifteen or twenty miles. It's easier with this stick." He paused. "It's a pretty good stick, but in the morning, I'll take that other one over there by the shed. It's an oak branch."

"I'm so damned cold!"

"When we get to Prague, I'll buy us a stove, Manny, and we'll get a good hot fire going inside... "

"My granddad used to sell stoves. Both my grandmothers had tremendous imaginations. They could imagine practically anything."

"You probably take after them, Manny."

"I'm cold from underneath," the second boy said.

"The ground's still pretty cold."

"It has no end, just a hundred beginnings."

"It can't last much longer, Manny."

"Remember how Leonard used to look forward to the springtime?"

"I think you were the one that was looking forward. Sometimes it's the opposite of what you really want. Like me, before I wised up to that Hungarian rabbi. I couldn't get used to the idea that a rabbi could look like he looked. But I was really trying to talk myself into it. Actually, it

66

wasn't the rabbi that mattered so much. It was me. I wanted to figure him out.''

The second boy shifted around to find a more comfortable position. He stared at his fingers. That made him think of those people from Gleiwitz. They'd eaten their own fingers to start with—that's what Frank Bondy said, anyway.

The night melted into the wind and fog. You could hear the rustling of trees and grass and wild animals.

"I just noticed some branches over there by that stump, Danny.''

"What good are branches, Manny?''

"We can cover ourselves with them.''

"All right, drag them over. But I'm not getting up on account of a few dumb tree branches. You can't get any warmth out of cold wood.''

The second boy dragged over a few that lay closest and piled them on top. The first boy could feel him shivering. They lay close, side by side, hidden under the branches. The forest made rushing noises, like waves.

*The second boy was remembering when they had finished their first shift at the munitions factory. They were in the camp at Meuslowitz in southern Germany then and they were allowed to take their first hot shower.*

*There was a mystery in bodies which made itself felt at certain times—moments they hadn't learned to anticipate. The mystery had to do with women, even if they were nowhere near, and also with each other. If they hadn't been so exhausted.*

*It was all the same, whether it was two boys' bodies or one, or if they were alone. All they had to do was think about a girl. One dark night, they were lying in the barracks after their shower, and suddenly the darkness seemed even darker than usual. They held each other tight to keep warm. They were freshly bathed and there was no need to shrink away from each other. For a few moments, something raged inside them both, a realization of what their bodies meant —beyond what they meant on the job or beyond the simple fact that they existed, the things they toyed with and didn't understand.*

67

*Danny had reached out his hand and touched Manny. Then he drew himself up in a ball. They were both naked. Manny lay there, curious to know what Danny would do next. Then Danny touched him with his mouth, as though he wanted to overpower all that darkness by meeting it half-way.*

*It was intuition which had darkened their minds, as though nothing else mattered. It was a combination of fear and hunger and desire.*

*By now they were exhausted. They were cold. Yet something had stirred inside him, reminding him fleetingly of that other time. They had slept afterwards, a light sleep, like forgetfulness, only it was half-forgetting and half-remembering. In the morning, before they left for the factory, they acted as though it had all disappeared with the daylight. That was so they wouldn't have to be ashamed of themselves.*

"Try to get some sleep, Manny, or we won't be worth a damn in the morning," the first boy said.

"My teeth are chattering," the other said.

"Forget it."

"You don't have as many teeth as I have, so they don't make so much noise."

"Forget it and go to sleep."

"I ache and itch all over."

"Don't be such a sissy."

"Danny, do you really think I knew about that tack?"

"Shut up, Manny, honest! Otherwise we won't be able to move in the morning. Forget it or we'll just exhaust ourselves and we'll die. If you start arguing about that tack, we can argue about a thousand other things."

"Are you scared?"

"Not of the dark or of the trees the way you are, Manny."

The first boy could feel how feverish he was. He warmed himself from the other boy's feverish body. He was drenched with sweat.

Manny tried imagining what it would be like if he'd set fire to the branches he'd piled on top of them. Or if somebody else would do it, without even knowing they were hidden underneath.

"Do you think anybody'll survive this, Danny? Do you think anybody'll live to see the summer?"

"You and I will, Manny."

The woods at night, the sky and tree branches overhead and the frost and mud below, looked strange and beautiful and unreal. It was as if it had nothing to do with them. But it did. This was where they were. They were there alone, like animals are alone and lost birds and trees and frost and stars. For awhile he listened again to the sounds the woods made.

"Remember that German foreman who had three sons in the Luftwaffe and lost them all? He told me one time that I reminded him of the son who was killed over London. He'd gotten a diamond-studded ribbon for bravery. He crashed his Stuka into some cathedral."

"One of those jelly sandwiches he used to bring in his lunch bucket would taste pretty good right now," the first boy said.

"Sometimes he'd bring two sandwiches instead of one, remember?"

Manny got up to get another branch, but then he threw it away. "Sometimes I remember some of those Germans who made things easier for us than they would have been otherwise. Jews and Germans are really pretty close, when you come right down to it. Probably because we've spent such a lot of time together. Sometimes I really feel encouraged that there are some Germans who don't go along with all this. They run as many risks as Jews do."

"You said something different this morning."

"It always cuts both ways, Danny." He tried to relax his stiff muscles and find a more comfortable position.

He thought about all the food he and Danny had scrounged and shared. And the food they hadn't shared. He thought of all the people who were hiding out tonight in other forests, somewhere else. Under the clouds and other stars, where the moon had a different shape. That brought his mind back to Frank Bondy.

"Sometimes I feel I am robbing and stripping other people when I think about them. You know what I mean?"

"Once we get there, I'm going to forget everything that's happened, Danny. And I'll kick anybody in the pants if they try to remind me."

"I'll remind you then. I'll sing you some Nazi songs."

"Things could be worse, Danny. The two of us know things could be a damned sight worse."

"You get over everything in time. You know what time does. As Frank used to say."

"For God's sake, aren't you going to sleep?"

"I don't know. I can't."

"Don't think about anything. Not even about Frank, Manny. I've already crossed Frank Bondy off my list for good. You've got a fever, but you'll be over it by morning. You're like a cat. We both are."

"I wouldn't even mind lying under a locomotive. I tried it once, Danny, at the ramp in Meuslowitz. The worst part is the leaking steam."

"We'll start on our way as soon as the sun comes up, Manny."

—Lying under a locomotive is better than dragging around rolls of sheet metal in the wintertime, Manny was thinking. Somebody always had to help him with the loads he couldn't manage.

"Do you remember that red-headed *pipl,* Manny?"

"Vaguely." He knew what Danny was going to say now.

"Remember when that little cherub asked me for some vaseline? He heard the people from the Czech transports might have some and he asked me to get some for him, that he'd give me as much bread and salami as I wanted the next Thursday."

"He just had a high opinion of Czech Jews, Danny. And he was pretty sure you still didn't know the difference between not having anything for supper *before* supper and afterwards. I also recall that you never saw any sign of that salami."

"And I went to a lot of trouble getting him that vaseline. At that time I didn't know there was practically *nothing* you couldn't get there. Like in any big seaport. I saw things I'd never seen or even heard of."

"Frank was the one who gave you the vaseline, I remember that much."

"He gave it to me because otherwise I'd have pinched it anyway."

"Skip it, Danny. Forget it."

"That kid wanted me to get him some more boys. He wanted me to do it too. He wanted me to do his recruiting. He had it all figured out. He was a smart little cookie. Later, Frank took him under his wing. He said it was nothing to be proud of, but that you shouldn't kick a man when he's down."

"Hell, Danny, I'm so cold, I can't fall asleep!"

"That red-headed kid was always so hungry, remember, Manny? Just like us, only different. He couldn't believe he'd last as long as the other *pipls*. He didn't have parents anymore. But while they were alive, they were glad he was a *pipl*. He was jealous of other boys. He was always worried about losing his looks, that he wasn't as cute and plump as when that German *kapo* picked him out. The *kapo* was in Birkenau on a murder charge. He'd been in jail before that, but since December 1933, he'd been kept in camps. He only kept his *pipls* until they were fifteen years old. When they reached puberty, he got rid of them. He couldn't stand hearing their voices crack. But that red-headed kid acted as if he didn't know that he and the rest of his *kapo's* harem were eating up our food rations. He brought other boys around as substitutes."

"Don't tell me you're feeling sorry for him, Danny?"

"Not one bit. I'm just saying that I can still remember how scared he was of getting skinny and ugly, being all skin and bones, or else getting too fat, that his ass would get too round or else it'd shrivel up. Then he was sure his old convict lover would let him go up the chimney one fine day at selection time."

"I hope that's what finally happened to him. How would that kid have gotten along in normal life?"

"He wanted to be irreplaceable. He wanted to be wanted.

71

But he knew he wouldn't be if he went around sticking out his same cute little fanny all the time or his sweet little mouth for that old convict, day after day."

"I know why he wanted to recruit other boys and I know why you're telling me about it too. You don't have to remind me there are worse places to be than a cold, windy forest at night."

"Better or worse," the first boy went on. "At first I thought the same rules applied everywhere."

"The two of us are different. You and me. We're better."

"Maybe. Sometimes."

"Maybe he really wasn't a faggot, Danny."

"He got sent to camp just like you and me. The only way he ever saw a girl was on the other side of the barbed wire. The *kapo* wangled him out of the showers after the first selection, when his parents got reprieved. He went into the gas chamber but because he was such a little kid and people were squeezed in so tight, the cyklon gas didn't filter down to him. That was when the *kapo* noticed him. They were clouting the little kids that didn't get gassed, so they could shove in another batch of people. The kid was lucky. He used to like to tell me about it. Maybe he wanted me to feel sorry for him. Maybe he was just bragging, though."

"We were older when they took us and we were lucky we were as strong as we were and that we were trained machinists. And that the *kapo* had a weakness for little red-haired boys."

"The kid told me what he needed that vaseline for. Apparently it doesn't hurt as much that way. But I never got one bite of salami from him. So I told him he was getting fat, that he was eating too much, just to worry him."

The second boy knew what was coming next. "You already told me how you hit him, Danny."

"Afterwards, I was scared to go back to the barracks for fear that *kapo* of his would come looking for me to get even."

"You already told me about it, but not in such detail. I thought the past was dead for you."

"It's not as dead as I wish it were. A lot of things *are,* though. I probably wanted to get this off my chest and that's why it keeps coming back." He stopped. "The kid went to the gas ovens on account of me."

"He had it coming to him, Danny."

"He wasn't so cute looking with no teeth. He knocked out my three front teeth, after I'd already knocked out his. But looking back, I still feel responsible."

"You don't have many teeth either."

"But I'll have a new set made, Manny."

"That little red-head didn't have to be a *pipl.* And he should have given you that salami when he promised it I don't think you need to feel responsible, Danny."

"I'm not too proud of myself."

"And you say *I'm* finicky!"

"I have a feeling a lot of those little *pipls* won't live through this."

"Forget it," advised the second boy. "The more you talk about it, the deeper into it you sink."

"I think that heel of mine's begun to fester," the first boy said.

"If you let it alone, it'll clear up by morning."

"We're lucky nobody ever took it into his head to make us into *pipls,* Manny."

"If I wasn't so cold and hungry, I probably wouldn't feel so bad right now."

# 7

They huddled close. It seemed as though the branches under which they lay were drawing off their body warmth.

"Frank used to remember things that never happened," the second boy remarked.

"I can remember forwards as well as backwards."

"Remember me telling you how my dad was in the Italian Dolomites during the First World War? He said the days were beautiful, too, but that it was freezing cold at night. Now I can believe him. There are a lot of things I believe only now, Danny, when people who told me about them are dead and gone. My dad brought back a mandolin from Italy. He paid a few pennies for it. The Germans took it."

"I often think about that little Hungarian rabbi. He lost 25 pounds in two weeks. His clothes were so big for him, he was scared they'd send him into the gas chamber. One time, while they were busy shooting Russians, they shoved us all in the barracks, pushing us right into the corners. The rabbi held on to me as if I was his own son. Then he started preaching to me."

"Danny, you know you were just talking when you told me everything's gone dead inside you."

"No, I wasn't just talking."

"So if it's dead, bury it all. At least on such a damn cold night. I'm dead tired."

"You were at the Buna Werke when that happened. I was with the little rabbi day and night. He used to tell me that God is the killer of little children. He wanted me to believe there's no God, that they'd done plastic surgery on him, that he's really the devil or a lunatic, at least, that it's all a fraud. He made me watch German soldiers selecting people to go into the gas chambers. Or watch at the family camp where parents would push their children ahead and where you saw sons hiding behind their fathers or a daughter behind her mother. Just so they wouldn't be the ones that got picked out. The rabbi wanted me to see how God splits one person away from another, making people into strangers, making them hate each other. But God does it so it looks like people do it of their own accord. God's testing us, he said, and we can resist. The worst part was, that little rabbi reminded me of my father after he went up the chimney. Like a smudge of soot. Then, Manny, that rabbi stole my bread ration!"

"If it wasn't so cold you'd never have thought about it. If you were feeling better, you wouldn't think about all those things. When that little rabbi stole your bread, he wasn't a rabbi anymore, he was just another mad man."

*The worst night was that time in September when his father went up the chimney. He was alone. He dreamed of Allied aircraft which would drop their bombs right into his bunk so that it would be clear, as clear as the clearest things: the alternation of day and night, the blowing wind, ice and snow. It was almost beautiful to imagine how a person would perish in a hundredth of a second, under the glowing core of the bomb.*

"I used to know a couple of gay cafes and baths in Prague. Do you suppose they're still there?"

"When we get that far and we're on our own, we can take the same name, Danny, what do you say? Like brothers. I'd like to be a pilot or drive a racing car. How about you? You said you would too."

The first boy pressed closer. They listened to the rustling of the forest. It came in waves enfolding the night and the two of them and everything else that was left over and other things which weren't there anymore.

"Remember that other German guard in the train when we hadn't had anything to eat for three days? And how he told us a person is what he eats? He didn't just invent that either."

"A person *is* everything. Also what he doesn't eat."

He realized that the two of them probably looked like a pair of crippled birds by now. And that the simplest thing of all would be to give themselves up. It was both good and bad that they were so alone, on the very fringe of existence, torn loose from everything else, so they could concentrate not only on their fight against exhaustion, but also against fear.

"It's dark here," he said after a little while. But he was thinking about something else.

They'd always be able to remember what it felt like to be cold and thirsty and hungry and scared. What warmth means and a roof over your head. A bed. A cup and plate and spoon. What it means, not being afraid of people or animals. Or the fact that we're all born of different mothers. For him, right now, looking backwards was a way of looking forward.

*He was walking Manya Cernovska home. She looked almost the same as she had three years ago. She told him how his parents' apartment had been confiscated as soon as they'd left. With everything in it. "They worked out a marvelous technique for taking over Jewish property," she told him. "For instance, after you left, they authorized dances to be held, but for Jewish young people only. Appar-*

77

*ently that was so nobody abroad could claim there was something wrong going on here. Then the Germans would come to these dances, with their wives and girlfriends, just so they could pick out whatever they liked that the Jewish boys and girls were wearing. It was like a fashion show. You can be sure your girls put on their best clothes and those German cows took their pick, even if they didn't usually confiscate the stuff immediately. Unless they were very impatient. They waited until the next day and then they did it according to a list which had all the necessary rubber stamps. That's how orderly the Germans are–scarves, brooches, rings or coats, evening skirts, blouses, elbow-length gloves–the kind you wear to dancing school–slippers, the sort of thing a girl is proud of, that makes her feel feminine."*

*"So they stole everything then."* He smiled and shrugged, as if there was no use talking about it.

*"They used different words,"* she explained. *"They said 'requisition' instead of 'steal'. Like turning your silk stockings inside out at night to air them."*

*"They stole away the meaning words used to have. It's like learning a whole new language in a strange new world. As if you can teach people to get used to anything–that you are and at the same time, you aren't, that you exist, and at the same time, you don't, that you're lying and telling the truth all together. I feel like I've come back from some other planet."*

*"If it were up to me I'd put them in a zoo, instead of all the vultures and hyenas,"* Cernovska said.

Afterwards, they spoke of pleasanter things. *"That camel's hair jacket with the darts at the side is very becoming on you, Manny,"* she told him. *"We ought to go out together more often. Can you imagine how lonely I used to be at the pool without you? Manny, listen, what happened to your mother?"*

He smiled gently, *"Don't ask me that."*

*"And your dad? And your little sister Anna?"*

*"They killed them."*

*"It's a miracle they didn't kill you too, Manny. Sometimes*

*I wonder why you didn't kill them back. So that every one
of your people that got killed, would take at least one of
them along with him."*

*"I don't know the answer. Maybe because nobody taught
my little sister in time how to kill somebody when you don't
want them to kill you back. It's different with grownups.
The best of us did fight back. Some of them are engraved
in my memory. They considered it was their first right to
defend themselves and their consciences too. Conscience
is like your heart–you can't carve off a piece and expect
the rest to function as before. For every one dead German,
the Nazis killed not ten, not a hundred, not a thousand,
not even ten thousand, but a hundred thousand of our people.
Old folks, men, women and children. Once the final bill
is added up, and when you take into account all the extenuat-
ing circumstances–and they won't be flattering for all the
Nazis' friends or enemies–there are going to be a lot of
folks who will have paid back what they got or who will
have hung on to what was taken from them. I'm not just
referring to those scarves and brooches either."*

*"That jacket really looks good on you, Manny. Look,
let's talk about something else, OK?"*

*"There was a lot I didn't know before, Manya. That's
understandable. But there's a lot that can't be explained.
I got to know some wonderful people. Better than I am,
but not as lucky as me and Danny and Frank Bondy. The
people who stuck it out the best are the ones who never
really believed in anything which might have just confused
them. They were the kind of people who take things as they
are."*

He'd forgotten how Frank used to say that things happened the way they did because there were such a lot of
fools among us.

*"Do you think anybody could come along now and say,
'Hey, Manny, take off that camel's hair jacket!' Do you
think you could ever go back to camp? Very few people
believed you'd ever come back. Some of them didn't even
want you to. Not because they wished anything bad for
you, but because if you did come back, their conscience
would bother them."*

79

"Danny, remember that morning in Poland before they put us on the transport for Germany?"

"Sure."

"We'd been in Auschwitz-Birkenau for almost a month."

"Yeah, well, so what?"

"We practically didn't know a thing about what was going on. In some ways it's good *not* to know. The more you know, the worse it is. You know what I mean? It was a beautiful sunny day. Nice and warm. That was the 26th day of the 28 we spent there. We left on the 28th, remember? That was a beautiful day too. The days that were most important for us, were always beautiful."

"I remember what the weather was like, but I don't remember much about the rest of it. I already told you that."

"It was on the 26th that the uprising started in the *Sonderkomando* in Crematorium Number 4."

"Well, I remember that, because all that day they shot at anybody who stepped out on the *Apelplatz*. A lot more people got killed than just those Germans the folks in the *Sonderkomando* managed to kill."

"They blew up Oven Number 4. That was tremendous. Nobody got burned in that oven anymore. Remember how tremendous it was? They even wrecked part of Oven 2 and Oven 3, according to what those Slovak prisoners told us afterwards. Apparently they'd mined it quite awhile before. They got the dynamite and fuse rope from those women in the F.K.L. who were finally hanged. They were waiting for the signal for some general mutiny. But nobody from the rest joined in the *Sonderkomando*. Everybody staged their own individual uprising. They were scared it would turn into a massacre. But if the people had joined in the *Sonderkomando,* the two of us probably wouldn't have left and we wouldn't be here. It's funny, isn't it, how everything is connected with everything else? And how a chance accident that kills one person, can save your life."

"I'm surprised you feel like talking about it."

"I do because it lasted such a short time. And because it was so wonderful. I simply couldn't believe it was possible

80

for somebody to do something like that. They stretched wires charged with electricity so as many people as possible could escape. But they were caught by the barbed wire and were shot like rag dolls. In the crossfire of three machine guns."

"They knew they'd be transferred the next day and be killed."

"Anyway..."

"It only took eleven minutes in Treblinka, according to what Frank found out from those Polish prisoners. And they'd been preparing it for years. Some uprisings only lasted a matter of minutes. It must be beautiful, a minute like that."

"The thing that Danish Jew did in the Little Fortress at Theresienstadt probably didn't take more than half of a minute."

"I remember him. That was beautiful too."

"Depends on what you mean by beautiful."

"It isn't just a matter of time. But time does play a certain role."

"What got you started on that?"

"Because we've been on our way for such a long time."

"It hasn't been such a long time, Manny."

"The fact we've been on our way for so long and on our own, must mean something. Know what I have in mind?"

"I couldn't care less."

"You don't know what I'm trying to say?"

"No."

"It'd be good if tomorrow would turn out to be a nice, sunny day."

"Maybe it will."

The second boy said no more.

He knew he wouldn't get warm by morning. *They warmed themselves some nights when they were working on the coal commando in Auschwitz-Birkenau, at the far wall of the crematorium.*

*The wall they worked beside was almost constantly warm. They could warm themselves by it only at night and at most,*

81

*for just a few minutes. Sometimes Manny pressed his cheek against the wall, then his chest, his thighs, belly, his whole body. Behind the wall, the fire roared, sounding as if some dead sun was burning there. Sometimes the two boys stood side by side, keeping warm. That was, really, the only benefit they gained from being in the coal commando—warm red bricks. They didn't have to speak. It was as if they had stolen the warmth. They knew they would be sorry if the wall got cold. And they knew there was only one reason why it never grew cold.*

"If I had a few matches, I'd light up this whole forest," he whispered.

"Then I'm glad you haven't got any," replied the first. "Who wants to get burned?"

"To warm up," said the second.

"We'll warm up, once we start walking."

"All the same, I'd like to light a match to it."

"Don't be crazy."

"For five minutes."

"Please, would you talk about something else?"

"Do you remember the last selection?"

*He thought about that father and his two sons. They stayed together for three weeks. And then when the first son started to get so horribly skinny, the father told him suddenly that they might not be staying together. He felt it in his bones, that because the Germans were going to be making a third selection, the three of them should separate. At least for a few days, until the first son got through it. "You want me to go the ovens?" the son asked. And the father in reply asked, "Do you want us all to go there?" So they remained alone. Many people were separated by fear. People are afraid to be together as well. Then they have nothing more to lean on. The first and last —children, mother, father—can change from being a support into a dead weight.*

"Are you trying to make me mad?" demanded the first boy.

82

The second one was silent. *Suddenly, inside his head, he heard the bombs start falling. The sun, in eclipse, cast a silver, aluminum light. The roaring of the B-17's was everywhere, like an echo. Like the time when he and Danny had been working in that munitions plant outside Dresden.*

The woods retreated.

*The first thing he and Danny did when the air raid started, was to open the foreman's locker and swipe two pairs of overalls, one clean, the other ready to be sent to the laundry.*

*The assistant foreman wore a black coat with a swastika on the lapels and he saw them do it. They knew he carried a pistol under his coat, even before he reached for it.*

*Danny had learned to judge people. Like an animal in the jungle who can recognise what's dangerous and what isn't.*

*He was holding a revolver, but Danny was already running with the overalls and Manny behind him. They ran into the next building as the 60 second sirens started, signalling a top emergency air raid. An enemy squadron had been spotted in Leipzig-Dresden air space and the assistant foreman had other things to do than to chase two pairs of stolen overalls.*

*The earth and air were filled with the noise of explosions. The factory was directly hit. There was earth and water and air and people—everything was filled with fear. People and houses and streets were aflame and even the Elbe River was on fire. Hardly any place was safe. Nevertheless, people stampeded toward the river and so did the two of them.*

*Besides bombs, the planes had dropped some kind of incendiary stuff which couldn't be extinguished. Nobody had ever seen anything like it. It made even asphalt and water burn. Houses burst into flame from top to bottom. Phosphorescent fires can be put out with sand, but the Germans would have needed a whole Sahara, plus twelve million more prisoners, to put out all those fires.*

*They watched rabbit hutches floating down the Elbe, sinking slowly, full of live rabbits.*

*There were thousands of people and there were probably
ten times that many huddled in the fields along the river-
bank. Then the aluminum bombers started to come back.*

Now, in the darkness of the forest, he could still see
those rabbits with their little pink eyes, drowning in the
Elbe. *The beautiful explosions began again, and then melted
into the rustling of the forest.*

*Frank Bondy said he guessed the Germans had learned
their lesson now. Some things are like hospitals: as long
as you don't need them, you couldn't care less, but just
as soon as you do, anxiety grabs you. "Like that famous
novelist always writes about," Frank recalled. "You know
the one I mean, boys."*

*They didn't, just as they didn't know what he was talking
about when he said, "the Jews will lose as long as they're
acrobats, the way they've always been so far, capable of
turning a defeat into the opposite, making a virtue out of
necessity instead of wiping out their enemies for a change.
Victory is just as much of a long term thing as defeat. You've
got to cultivate both for at least 300 years—like an English
lawn or all the tears that flowed in Bohemia after the battle
of the White Mountain."*

*"You know when I was 100 percent wrong, boys?" Frank
went on. "When I said I was done with making do, with
what's just temporary."*

*The people from Kohen's bunch, said Frank, didn't make
much sense. He was locked into an invisible circle made
of all his memories of past sins and satisfactions which
improved in retrospect. In jest, he once said that under
normal circumstances, a baker making buns in Prague is
just as useful as a businessman in New York City with
all his stocks and bonds. "What do you suppose makes
the biggest fools out of people?" he demanded. "You can
have three guesses." He never gave the answer. That was
one of many things he only hinted at.*

*Then also a lot of children, women and men burned to
ashes—though never as many as in Auschwitz—and Frank*

84

*counted himself among those who wished it on them. Maybe it looked different, watching it from behind camp wires, than from Berlin or from the bombers. Maybe it looked more elegant from above. But only those who were risking their necks by flying here, really knew whether it was just and fair or not–and those who were behind the camp wires and who, every day and every second for the past three years, had been in the shoes of those people who were on fire down there. Maybe the ones who started it all and who were now on fire too, ought to have known to begin with what was fair and what wasn't.*

Bombs, Franks' maxims, the flaming river and the drowning rabbits with their pink eyes—they all floated up through the murmuring treetops.

# 8

He felt like he was lying on a wet anthill. He didn't know whether he'd been asleep or not. Danny was holding onto him with two hands, the way a baby clings to its mother, breathing close against his cheek. His left leg was bent.

"What time do you suppose it is?" whispered the second boy.

"I don't know. It's not morning yet," the first boy mumbled drowsily. "You can't see the stars."

"You said we'd get an early start, Danny."

"We'd bump into trees when it's as dark as this. We'd just get lost."

"I rested a little bit."

"Yesterday really did us in. It's cold. And awfully damp."

"When it's dark I have all sorts of funny visions."

Slowly the sky turned grey as day began. The first boy pushed aside the branches they were covered with.

"The visions have gone. I saw them all, though, real close this time."

"How's the fever, Manny?"

"All I need to do is lie down and close my eyes and I see them. I can cope with it better in daytime. If I lie down, it all passes in front of my eyes."

"It's not just your imagination, Manny. That's normal. That's the way it is. You can bet your neck on that."

"Or my feet."

"But not both. Someday you're bound to strike it lucky."

"It's getting light."

"It doesn't look as if it's going to rain."

"How come I never see you cry, Danny? Don't you ever cry?"

"Do you really want to know, Manny?" He paused. "When we went to the transport, my dad was working on a Jewish construction team, building barracks for the SS in Prague. My mother and sister and I had to go on ahead to Theresienstadt. They promised they weren't going to split up families. That was the first time I ever saw my dad cry. He was scared he'd never see us again. And it was too late to do anything about it. Except we could have all gone into the kitchen and turned on the gas. He told Mother to look after us, then he hugged her and kissed us kids. He stayed on in our old apartment. Some of the lady neighbors were probably pleased he was by himself. Then the apartment was confiscated. We were finally reunited, but then they separated us again. It would have been better if he hadn't cried that time."

"People remember some things for a long time."

"Dad was like a god to me for years. Then he just watched us go away and suddenly it stopped for me. I was surprised he could let us go like that."

*Frank wanted them to fetch a blanket or a piece of canvas from the factory for that Polish girl so he could give it to her and she could protect herself against the winter. They told him it was out of the question. He told them that basically, it all boils down to wanting to enough. He had four rules:*

*First, you fight because you want to win. Second, you realize you can't win, but you keep on fighting anyway because it's important not to give in. Third, you fight from habit, because you've been taught to; you're used to it and it's expected of you. Fourth, if you don't put up a fight, you're lost.*

*Finally they found him an old burlap bag which he presented to her as if he were holding a bridal train.*

"Those Transcarpathians felt sorry for Frank. As if they knew he'd cave in before it was all over."

"They thought they were immortal, just like Frank did, because they all believed in the same things. But if Frank died along with them, maybe they really *are* immortal now, huh, Danny?"

"The guards probably shot them fast and didn't even bother to haul them off to make soap out of."

The second boy said nothing.

"Sometimes Frank acted like a little god. Like my dad. I was just waiting for him to crack up, though. With all those superstitions of his."

Now the second boy didn't even answer. As if the attack on Frank Bondy had actually been directed against him. He could imagine why, and yet, at the same time, he couldn't imagine everything. More than anything else, Danny always depended on his own strength, his own will and his own luck. When one of these failed him—in the night, in the wound in his heel—he wanted to patch things up with Frank before they started going again, even though Frank might already be dead.

"He was like a submarine. When a possibility emerged, he came to the surface to show what he knew. If the goal faded, he went down under the water, again, but never for very long. He just waited for another chance."

Danny paused. "His hopes were like a submarine, too. He thought some miracle would happen, and in the end everything would be OK."

The second boy didn't answer.

*He and Danny had been hauling coal for the kitchen. All six crematoria were processing the transports from Galicia and Transylvania. So the pressure on the rest of the camp had eased up for a few months.*

*A high-ranking commission from Berlin had come to visit the camp commander. Twice a day, he made his welcome speech: "Go take a bath, Jews. I know how you feel. I know what you've missed most on your way here. After all, we're only human too. I promise you the water will be nice and warm. We don't want to deprive you of comforts you're accustomed to. Undress quickly. You're among soldiers here, this is not a health resort. We expect all of you to work. You can't wage a war without discipline and we want to win. We'll be able to get along with anybody who understands that. But we also know what to do with anybody who refuses to understand. Save water. Turn on the water, soap up, stop the water again and only then rinse yourself off. Someone else's turn will come after yours and they want to get just what you did. Now then: women separately to my right, men to my left. Children under 14 and men and women over 40 remain in the middle. Each person is to hang his belongings on one single hook. Shoes and whatever you have in your pockets are to be neatly arranged under your clothes hook so there will be no mix-up when you come back. Today, as an exception, towels will be handed out after you finish bathing. Also, the delivery of soap has not arrived yet. Therefore you're getting one bar of soap for every four people. I apologise for that. But the water's nice and warm. The boilers are heated up. Now then, you have two minutes . . . "*

*Everything ran smoothly, Mothers and fathers, their children and other groups, proposed each other. The dressing rooms were separated by a high lattice.*

*A tall commissar and his escort stepped over to the round window that was set in the open door of the shower rooms, like a porthole on a boat. In front of him was a devout man from the East, with his wife and seven children.*

*"That man is the epitome of everything Jews like that believe in."*

The tall commissar merely nodded.

"It's part of their belief which apparently cannot be extinguished by gas or burned away by fire," the commander added. "They believe smoke comes out of his nose and flames from his mouth. Actually, they might be right in a few minutes."

The devout man had three black-haired sons and four red-haired daughters. They were shaven now. The man's beard had not been cut off. Otherwise, all of them were naked and shorn. The youngest held the soap in his hands and looked it over in such a way as if he had never held such a porous cake of soap in his life, with ÜVA-DU and a number stamped distinctly on it.

The old folks behind them were their parents and grandparents. They looked down because they were ashamed.

The bearded man was silent. Then he uttered a single word. It was inaudible from the outside.

"The thing they fear most about gassing," went on the commander, "is that we'll separate them from the members of their families. And so in most cases, we leave them together. They think if they remain together, things won't go to extremes. As long as they remain together, the notion of a final solution simply escapes them. And then, when it dawns on some of them, they're glad that at least they're all together and that the final solution is fairly shared among them. Every family unit is like a ship that's going to the bottom and on board to start with, everybody encourages everybody else that they won't necessarily drown, and even if they do, at least they'll all perish. As though that really made things any easier.

The commander was sharing his observations with the tall commissar without knowing he could be heard on the other side of the wall.

"With transports of whole families, the liquidation process moves much quicker than with transports composed of more heterogeneous units. They probably believe families have some special protective powers. It's enough to keep them together and they're in no condition to believe that this is the last stage in the final solution. It's enough, a

91

*day or two before the final solution, to give them—at expense of the ones who are still living—an extra slice of bread or salami, a change of underwear, let them sleep a little longer or order the medic to give them some vitamin C and they see this as a total confirmation of their belief that they'll soon be going back to where they came from. They never believe we want to kill them. They aren't capable of understanding this. Finally, they don't even believe what gets whispered around within their own ranks. And every day, every hour we let them live, every slice of bread, every bowl of porridge, every shoelace and stitch of underwear we give them, induces them to believe something other than what is really waiting for them. They come here like sheep, with only a few exceptions. A kind word does more than army units whose weapons we can make better use of on other fronts."*

*Now both of them starred into the chambers. Some of them inside were praying. The smallest were clamoring that they didn't want to die, as though they were confronting the final solution for the first time. It looked ridiculous from the outside, the foolish way they clung to life, from the youngest to the oldest.*

For five minutes, the first boy tried to hammer out the tack with a stone. Then he inspected his festering heel. Finally he stretched. Both boys were stiff after lying all night on the hard ground, under the rough branches.

"I feel like I haven't slept more than a second," Manny said.

# 9

The first boy got up slowly. He could feel a sticky pain in his foot which he had not felt when he was lying down, and it was worse than the day before.

Snow still lay in the sheltered parts of the woods. That afternoon they didn't say a word about the weather. After a few hours, the tip of the tack had worked itself through again. Perhaps the heel was so worn down, or the leather was so soft that the tack would come through again and again.

Danny was playing hide and seek with the pain in his foot. The pain had shades.

The stick he'd picked up in the feeding shelter helped him. The woods looked different in the silence, without the rain. He leaned on both sticks.

And then the other said, "Remember that strong Slovak from the *sonderkommando* and how that friend of his told him they were going to send his mother to the gas the next day and whether he couldn't do something for her? And how he told him, 'We all have mothers'? In other words, he was telling him everybody had mothers, not only him. And the other guy just kept looking at him so the strong Slovak said, 'If you look at me that way one more time, I'm going to take a piece of iron and hit you over the head with it so you won't ever look at anybody that way again. Where do you think we are? What do you think I can do? I wasn't able to do anything even for my own mother and the only thing my friends did for me was to put me on the second shift. And lock me up in the storeroom. Do you want me to do that to you? When are they taking her?' And that friend of his told him the selection was supposed to be the next morning. Finally the Slovak offered to do the only thing he could think of for his friend. 'Do you want me to get you into the showers along with her? That's really all I can do for you.' And he was surprised to discover that he probably would have been glad if anybody had made him that offer when his own mother had been gassed.''

"The strangest things always stick in your mind, Manny.''

"What's strange about it?''

"Why do you keep looking back? Why do you always keep turning around and looking back, Manny? A person'd think you don't believe in where we're going.''

"That's just it, I do believe in it. When I turn around and look back, it's like I'm saying to everything, 'so long, every thing—now I know about you, but in a couple days or in a week from now, I'm starting a new life and I'm going to want to start it without you.' ''

"I don't suppose those things you're talking about, could care less.''

"But it's a fact, all kinds of stuff keeps coming into my head, things that are perverted and normal, all at the same time.''

"I'm thinking about the clothes I'm going to buy when we get to Prague, Manny. And the shoes.''

"I like thinking about that too, Danny.''

"I've got an imagination like a girl, Manny.''

"Me too. I know a couple shops in the Sterba Arcade. And on Perlova Street. I know just where they sell all kinds of good-looking clothes."

"Don't forget to get de-loused before you try on all those good-looking clothes."

"I never knew how many times a person has to get de-loused," the second boy said.

He was so tired by now that he didn't feel like thinking over all the reasons why the other boy didn't talk about the pain in his foot.

*He remembered something Frank had said once, when they caught him telling some little white lie that nobody even minded anymore. 'What are we supposed to do,' he said, 'when we live in a world where even your best friends lie because everybody lies and lying is part of a person's character just like it was once the thing to do to tell the truth?' And he'd smiled gently and sadly and at least his lies didn't seem so crude. Like when people knew what was going to happen to somebody, but they told him, 'Hi, how are you?' or 'We'll see you this evening,' even when they all knew they'd never see each other again. And it wasn't only in front of the shower room or on the ramp at the station or on the way from one camp to another.*

*They'd learned it in the German camps but, as Frank said, there had been some important prerequisites for it even before. It was the same thing with cowardice as it was with lying and with a whole lot of other things.*

*Danny acted like the cards were rigged, so he simply wasn't going to play the game, even though a lot of other people were playing and maybe that was why they all used to stick up for Danny before. Manny remembered that there was a time when they'd stick up for him too a little, for the same reason. Was that why Frank had befriended the two of them?*

*Then they finally learned that the best thing was to adjust to whatever it is that pains you because there were always other sides to it, like everything else.*

*So he simply didn't talk about the nail in his shoe, as*

95

*if talking about it and about the wound in his heel might
kill him.*

Most of the way was downhill. Yesterday, it had been
uphill. The second stick was an encumbrance, so Danny
tossed it away and leaned on the other, using it like a crutch.

Occasionally the second would look up into the treetops.
He was thinking about bird's nests and eggs. —March is
too early for birds' eggs.

There were old cobwebs hanging from the lower branches
of the trees, ragged from the rain and snow and wind. Dead
cobwebs.

Later that afternoon, a fox ran across their path. The
sky grew overcast. The edge of the forest kept disappearing
before them. The goal they had set for themselves got further
away, the closer they got.

"I can't see the sun anymore," the second boy said.

"We're headed east. West is over there."

"We'd save ourselves a lot of detours if we were on a
road."

"That depends on where we are, Manny. We're still deep
inside German territory."

"This slows us down, having to climb all the time."

"Look, I can assure you that I'm not exactly in love
with these woods either."

"If we were on a road, we could hitch a ride on a wagon
that was going in our direction."

"You're beginning to smell pretty bad," the first boy said,
changing the subject.

"Prague... " the second boy mused. "How far away
do you think it is?"

"As my mother used to say, ask me no questions, I'll
tell you no lies."

"Do you want to keep going till it gets dark, Danny?"

"We'll go just a little farther."

"How far? It's dark already."

"At least to the top of the hill in front of us, Manny,
OK?"

96

They plodded grimly on, side by side. The first boy was limping badly.

"Don't you feel well?" asked the second boy.

He was obviously scared of an answer, yet he expected it.

"No," the first boy replied.

"Are you sure moss grows on the north side of the tree trunks?"

"The wind whistles like a tea kettle, huh, Manny?"

"I've got belly cramps."

"I had the same thing yesterday."

"My eyes are swelling up."

"Just this one last hill and that's it for today, Manny."

"The sun's set already. There's no sense going on."

"Those are hunger cramps. It's nothing serious."

"You mean I'm being a sissy?"

"Among other things."

"How far have we come today?"

"I didn't keep count."

"What were you counting, then?"

"Steps."

"You want to keep going in the dark, Danny? I'm one big bruise."

"You and me both, Manny."

"You should have taken off that shoe as soon as it started to hurt."

"And go barefoot?"

"How far shall we go?"

"I saw a clearing on the far side of the hill. Right at the top."

"Hold on to me, Danny."

"Nobody could have thought up a forest that goes on as long as this one."

"I'll see if I can find some water. So you can wash up, at least."

"Where are you going to find water in the dark?"

"I wish I knew where we are."

"We're over the worst, that's for sure. Things already start to look familiar."

"Yeah, now just tell me you want to do this all over again when the war's over."

The first clung to the second boy's arm. They were both limping. Manny was remembering how many times he'd been lucky. And thinking how nothing lasts forever. Like Frank used to say: "Life gives happiness only to some folks, and it's never for keeps. Like stations where you change trains for somewhere else."

"Just this last stretch, then you can tell me to go to hell if you want to, Manny."

It was not quite dark when they came to the edge of the clearing. Then the moon broke through the clouds.

"This is what Frank was talking about," said the second.

The first slumped beside the feeding shed, as though he couldn't believe his eyes. Before he sat down, he put his stick where he'd found it that morning.

"This makes me sick," said the second.

"It was the sun that got me mixed up," the first said softly. "That lousy, fucking sun, Manny." After a while, he went on. "And those hills that zigzagged back and forth. We were hardly able to take more than a couple of steps in a straight line, right, Manny?"

"Aw, it's OK, Danny."

The second lay down on the branches beside the shed, which were just where they'd left them that morning.

The first boy was thinking how the sun had fooled him, along with the mountains and his own feet and their bellies. He felt as if he'd been hit over the head with a blunt instrument. But he hardly had enough strength to put it into words.

The second boy lay staring off into the forest. In the dusk, the space between the trees looked like tunnels; they reminded him of the canals the Polish women at Meuslowitz had told them about; the tunnels were they'd been captured. For the first time it occurred to him that they weren't going to make it. He hadn't strength enough to blame it on Danny. And yet, inside he did. He shivered and tried hugging himself and curling up in a ball. He wasn't listening to what Danny was trying to say about the sun.—You can't get all the way to the end. Woods are even worse. They don't just go in one direction either. The stench of canals and stagnant water was in his nostrils. And mucky puddles. The breath of old grass and earth. A sharp reek. For a moment the woods were red as blood.

Like the first boy, he ached all over. They were going to die here by this game refuge. They would soon be eaten up by insects and mice and foxes and wolves. The squirrels would nibble at them. Before they rotted away. Danny's skeleton . . . In his tired brain, red went white. Bones were white.

He lay there, inert, as though even his tongue was powerless. He could see and hear every move and every friction of Danny's bones. He didn't even feel like trying to move his tongue to see if it would work.

He tried to lift his eyes to the treetops, to see whether he had any will-power. He strained his ears in a conscious effort to hear the sounds of the forest. Those other sounds that accompanied his visions had come back. Things he'd heard. His bones. The sewers turned back into trees again.

The wind had uprooted all the trees and piled them where the two boys lay. He breathed heavily. They were not in some new, strange part of the forest—they had just come back to where they had been before. He pulled over a branch and covered his head with it. He lay in almost the same trough his body had made the night before. The place was crawling with insects, red and white and translucent. He wished they'd go away.

The first boy waited until the second fell asleep and then he took off his shoe, hissing with pain.

But the second boy wasn't really asleep. He wondered why Danny hated Frank so much. When people start hating someone, it's because they're a lot alike.

He could see tree branches above him. He could see them even when he closed his eyes. The trees seemed to be falling on his head.

He could hear them crashing down on him. Silver, black and pungent, heavy trees, illuminated and magnified by the moonlight. They fell slowly like a man trying to escape something and not being able to.

99

As they fell, the trees stirred up a tempest of sound, like a glider coming in for a landing. They whispered as they fell on his head, like before the war when workers brought bundles of Christmas trees into town and tossed them onto the pavements.

He watched three trees fall on him after he opened his eyes. He couldn't dodge them and he hadn't strength enough to warn Danny.

"We've got to go in the other direction tomorrow," the first boy said.

The sun was high. They walked side by side. The first boy leaned on the other's shoulder and on his stick. They looked like two sick, skinny wolves. Their eyes were bloodshot and the corners of their eyes and mouths were caked with white. There were sticky patches of resin on their clothes and both were scratched and bloodied by the underbrush.

"We've got to get out of these woods," the first boy said. When the second boy did not answer, he went on, "Don't be a bastard, Manny." No response. "I bet they'd trade places with us if they could. I hope you're not planning to put on that act again when we are almost at the top of the hill."

The second boy didn't even look up. The first was worried about him. Manny stopped and leaned against a tree.

"I've seen where the woods end," the first said. "All right, Manny, if that's the way you want to be, I can be just as much of a skunk as you can." He waited. "As long as I can remember, you've always wanted to die like that Danish Jew. Remember, Manny?"

The second boy looked off toward a clearing, but it wasn't where the forest ended. It was just a stony place where no trees grew and beyond it the woods began again. His eyes were gummy.

Danny's lips barely moved when he spoke. "So far, you've never let yourself get tramped on, Manny. All we have to do is get across this patch of stones." He leaned on his stick.

"How long has it been since we've had anything to eat?" asked the second boy.

"There's no sense keeping count all the time."

"I'm staying right here."

"I'll scrape something up today. The woods are different here. I swear, Manny."

"You said the woods end here."

"It's a different kind of forest, Manny. It's not the same anymore."

"You won't find us anything to eat," said the second boy.

With the aid of his stick, the first boy began to pick his way across the patch of rocks. He looked back occasionally, but most of the time, he peered around for a place to put his stick. He foundered over the stones, step by step, assuming Manny would follow him.

The second boy finally moved away from the tree where he'd been leaning.

"There must be a cave around here," Manny said dully.

"Inside your belly, maybe," replied the first boy.

They floundered on. The first boy knew what it would mean if he were to fall now. If that medic-amputator were still alive, he would have gleefully volunteered to cut off his festered foot and then he'd be able to hobble along on one leg, with the aid of his faithful stick.

Achingly, he wished they would make it. He turned around, "Manny!"

The second boy had fallen and lay face down on the stones. Danny went back to help him, but he had to be careful not to fall too.

"All right, go on, just lay there and let yourself get shot at. That's your best chance," he whispered.

Blood trickled from the cut on Manny's forehead. He had fallen against a sharp stone. The wind rose and brought with it the first drops of rain. Danny brushed away the pine needles from his face.

The second boy turned his head. The stone was cool against his cheek. The blood felt warm and sticky.

He could hear Danny talking to him and, vaguely, he

101

thought about all the people he had disappointed—Frank and his mother and himself. All of the people he'd ever known.

It began to rain and the rain washed the blood off his forehead and off the stone. The first boy stood there looking back at him. Manny was vaguely aware of his own exhaustion.

He looked past Danny, between the trees and beyond the patch of rocks. He could see branches and cobwebs that looked like streaming rope ladders which had been ripped apart by the wind and mended. He was sure there must be spiders there, waiting for bugs to come along, and he was the bug they were waiting for. He hoped they wouldn't gnaw his eyes out. The rain drummed against his head, bouncing off the stones and into his eyes.

Danny hobbled back and poked him with his stick.

"Sit down," the second boy said.

"I wouldn't be able to get up again," replied the first. "It's full of varmints down here."

"You're bleeding a little," the first boy said. "You must have hit your head on a sharp stone."

"Wait, Danny."

Finally, leaning against each other, they tottered arm in arm across the rocky patch.

# 10

"Horses have been this way," said the first boy when they came to a path in the forest.

"A year ago, it looks like," replied the second. His hair was matted.

"What's wrong with your eye?"

"It feels swollen. When I close it, it's like going to the movies."

"What are they playing today, Manny?"

"I can see a naked woman made out of stone. She's sitting up above the fountain at the top of Wenceslaus Square. When you stand below and look between her legs, you can see street cars."

"You and Frank must have been related."

"I can't remember how I fell and cracked my head," the second boy said.

*He was remembering the time in Meuslowitz when Frank
Bondy had invited him and Danny to his kapo room. He
asked them to sit down, as if they knew what he had on
his mind. They'd been planning an escape and Frank said
it would be a milestone in his life.*

*It was enough to listen to his deep and pleasant voice.
It made you feel it was a privilege, just to be with Frank
Bondy. He told them about his past, so they'd realize what
an honor it was to escape with him.*

*For instance, the three chairs which Frank had found
somewhere so that he could invite both of them to sit down.*

*Speaking of their escape plan, Frank said their first duty
was to get the key to the gate leading into the women's
section. He explained it so it made sense, saying the elec-
trified barbed wire in the women's camp was strung high
where it ran through boggy land.*

*"I'd be happy if only this once, the devil would work
for us," he smiled. It looked as though anybody would drown
if they tried to crawl under the wire. But nobody had ever
tried.*

*There was no guard beside the bog. The muck was deter-
rent enough.*

*That evening, the boys took an imprint of the keyhole
with a piece of soap Frank had given them. Danny stole
some old keys in the factory. He filed down one of them
from the imprint. On the fourth day, they tried it. It fit.
They gave it to Frank.*

*A few days later, they found out that with the help of
their key, Bondy was going to see his Polish girlfriend whose
name was Wanda. She worked in the kitchen. She'd gone
through the sewer experience like most of the Polish women
in camp and like most of them, she was a devout Catholic.
Almost all of them had been raped by German soldiers
when the prison train had stopped on the way to camp.*

*Frank Bondy had his mouth full of apologies the next
day, but each new day was an accusation too, and so was
every word they used to try to convince him to forget the
Polish bitch. They were jealous of that poor Polish girl who'd
fallen head over heels in love with Frank. She gave him*

104

*food, anxious to erase through him everything that had happened to her.*

*It was Wanda, oft-raped, shorn-headed, who seemed to be the main obstacle to their escape.*

*That was when Frank gave the boys the address of his fiancée in Prague in case anything happened to him while they were making their escape. Danny was to have his watch and his money was to go to Manny.*

*Frank had remembered his fiancée in Prague even when he was with Wanda. He wrote letters to her, telling her how much she meant to him and he told the same thing to the Polish girl. He wasn't lying to either one. He used to say, "Each story has three versions. The first one you tell me. The second one I tell you, and the third one no one knows."*

"Bondy-boy was just a fancy fake," said the second boy. "Why do you keep thinking about him all the time?"

"I don't. I'm just thinking in general. How do you suppose he got along with his girlfriend in Prague?"

"Probably like a cat and a rat," replied the first. "I've dethroned Frank Bondy long ago. Like I did with my dad when the Germans came. Even though it wasn't *his* fault."

"The grass is slippery."

"Hold on tight!"

"As long as you don't eat my fingers when I grab you."

Suddenly the path led out into a field. They stopped by a tall thicket. A man was pushing a plow blade into the earth as his horse plodded across the field.

Hidden in the thicket, they watched the plowman lead the bay horse where the land sloped toward a cluster of houses from where a woman had just come. She was bringing the man his lunch.

"We'll have to kill that woman," the first boy said. "Otherwise she'll turn us in."

The man was unshaven. He wore a motley collection of clothing topped with a ragged, high-collared army overcoat.

105

The woman waited for the man to eat his lunch. The woman was pretty. The man must have been at least a generation older than she. She wore a woolen cap, woolen stockings and a pair of high laced man's shoes.

While the man ate, the woman watched the horse and the sky and the drifting clouds. He bit and chewed and swallowed, watching the woman.

She turned away.

"How'll we kill her?" whispered the second boy.

"With a rock or with my stick," replied the first.

"Who's going to do it?"

The man had the horse's bridle in one hand and a slice of bread in the other.

The boys watched and swallowed hard. When the man had finished eating, he bent down for the jug. It was full of milk. It trickled along his chin to his neck and down his chest.

The woman stood there, staring dreamily into space. Her black hair was combed back smoothly under a flowered kerchief. When the man had finished eating and drinking, he smiled at her and the woman picked up the jug, wrapped it in a kerchief and slipped it into her bag.

Slowly, she walked back the way she had come. She took long strides, holding herself erect, as though she knew the path by heart.

Up on the hillside, the man went back to plowing the spring earth. The woman did not look back. The unshaven plowman worked slowly, his steps following the lazy plodding of the horse. As he turned the heavy, soft earth, it cast its reflection back against his face, muddy and black.

The woman came to the edge of the village and went into a house with a red roof. This was just a little cluster of houses; the main part of the village was on the other side of the hill. There was a shed built onto the house, a hay rick and an outhouse.

A German shepherd dog with a long chain rushed out of its dog house, welcoming the woman with wild barking. For the first time, the woman smiled. Somewhere beyond the village, somebody's bitch barked in response, a long wailing bark.

After awhile, the woman opened the door and went into the yard. She was wearing a black dress and apron. She scattered grain to the hens. The dog barked and the woman smiled again, at the dog, at the hens and to herself.

"It looks like she's alone," the first boy said.

"How do you want to do it?" asked the second.

"Just one of us is going to have to do it, Manny."

"Which one?"

"We'll draw lots," the first said. "Choose a number from one to twenty, Manny. But hurry!"

"Fifteen," the second said. His eyes glittered. "Start with me."

The first boy counted off. "It's you, Manny," he said. His breath was hot and rank. "You've got to kill her."

"OK., I will."

"If you don't do it to her, they'll do it to us."

"Yeah. Lend me that stick. I'll kill her as soon as she gives me something to eat."

"But before you do, make her tell you where we are and how far we've got to go."

When the woman finished feeding her chickens, she took a lump of sugar from her apron pocket. She let the dog jump around her for awhile. Finally she tossed him the sugar. The dog jumped high, snapped at the sugar and gulped it down.

The air was fragrant with the smells of the forest, the meadows, of early spring and the warm cowshed. The second boy narrowed his eyes and pressed his lips tight, trying not to think about food. The door to the shed was open. It wasn't possible to see inside. It was a clear darkness, underscored by the light after the rain.

A bell in the village began to toll noon. Pigeons flapped from one rainspout to another. A rooster crowed in the chicken coop. The first boy looked at the open door of the shed.

"How about burning the whole place down to be sure?" suggested the first.

107

"It would be a lot of work. I'm not strong enough. Anyway, how? Why? Do you suppose that would keep her busy until we could get away?"

The first boy kept looking at the shed.

"If you can run fast."

"I can't run."

"OK."

"I wouldn't leave you in that fix," said the first boy at once. The second boy didn't reply.

The woman went into the cowshed and when she reappeared, she had that same musing smile they couldn't make out. She didn't close the door to the shed.

"Get her to tell you how far it is to the nearest town," repeated the first. "I'll wait here."

"Wait by the woodshed."

"Don't take too long, Manny."

"You can wash your foot at the pump there, Danny."

"Most important, get rid of her."

"Don't worry, I will kill her."

"No matter what, Manny."

"Yeah."

The second strode off alongside the woodshed, holding the first boy's stick to keep the dog away. He'd forgotten how long it had been since he and Danny had had anything to eat.

Suddenly he stopped and turned his head. "I don't know what it is, but I'm not hungry anymore."

The woman was standing by the dishpan. She looked up startled when the boy entered the room with the stick in his hand. Horror flickered in her eyes.

The boy glanced swiftly around the room. A two year old child was under the table. The woman had a cool, pretty face and tidy hair. The child crawled out from under the table and clutched the mother's hand. The hand was trembling.

The boy was surprised by the impression he had made. He knew he must look frightful and that he'd be scared too if he could have seen himself. He raised the stick and approached the woman, who almost fainted. She was unable to utter a single sound. Even if she could have, she probably would have been afraid to scream, because then it would just happen faster.

But her fear was not transmitted to the child, "She can think anything she wants to," the second boy said to himself. He closed the door behind him, but otherwise he did not move.

He saw the fear of death in her eyes and the satisfaction he felt was different from what he expected.

He knew he only needed to take three or four steps with his lifted stick and it would be all over. He simply hadn't been prepared for the child. The idea of killing the woman had come simply; it had been much easier than when he had tried to understand *why* the Germans were killing his people who hadn't harmed them in any way.

—I'll take three and a half steps. I'll hit her over the head as hard as I can. When she falls, I'll hit her a few times more. What'll I do when the kid starts bawling?

Just as he knew he had the right to kill the woman, he knew he shouldn't kill the child and that he wasn't going to. But he couldn't put the two things together. He wondered what to do about the child. He could tie her to the table and lock the door. He saw a kitchen cupboard similar to what they had at home, with grey pottery cups. The chair-backs had angular carvings.

A blue tin bread box stood on the table next to the dishpan. His eyes shifted to it for a split second and the woman's followed.

Beside the bread box lay a long butcher knife. It was within the woman's reach. The second boy figured he could bar her way if she took one step. But meanwhile he had to lean his back against the door so he did not fall.

The table beside which the woman and the little girl were standing was covered with an old-fashioned, fringed white cloth with another of red linen on top of that. There was a sofa against the wall with an embroidered sampler showing a cook with a forest warden and some German proverb.

On the cupboard, stood a kerosene lamp with a white shade. Beside the sink hung a porcelain coffee mill with a wooden handle. Opposite the cupboard there stood an antique clock with signs of the zodiac, gilded Roman numerals and hands of blue tin. The clock ticked loudly. It was a quarter past two. The woman carefully turned off the spigot, stopping the water that had been running into the dishpan, now almost overflowing. The room was silent.

The woman turned to shield the child. She still couldn't move because of fear. He looked around the room as if it were an island. The place was very clean.

—So this is how people live, he thought to himself. With all this stuff. God, it's impossible! They have everything even in the midst of war.

"What do you want?" the woman finally asked in German.

"Something to eat," he replied.

The woman moved aside in that same, careful, dreamy way. Pulling her hand out of the child's grasp she opened the bread box and took out half a loaf of fresh bread. Holding it against her breast, she picked up the knife and cut three slices. Then she put the bread back.

The second boy could smell the bread and the room. He watched her lay the slices of bread on the table so he could take them. He was dizzy. He narrowed his eyes and the woman saw murder in them. He imagined himself taking three swift steps forward, hitting her over the head, then finishing the job as she lay on the floor, her skirt twisted so he could see her garters.

He had to fight back the dizziness. He leaned against the kitchen door. He stood facing the clean, neatly-dressed German woman and her blond, blue-eyed German child in the room to which the plowman returned each day when his work was done—was he her husband or her father? Blood rushed to his head and flooded his eyes.

He reached out and took the bread. The woman put her hands on the child's head. He raised the stick. It was his bloodshot eyes she noticed most.

"I have nothing more to give you," the woman told him.

The second boy was silent.

"No lard, no margarine," added the woman.

The second boy moved into the doorway, holding the

bread against his chest. The woman was petrified with fear. Although he knew he wasn't going to do anything to her. Within him roared the word 'thank you' just as a flaming sea would roar. But he didn't say a single word. Beneath the dirt, his face was flushed with blood.

The first boy was waiting for him by the woodshed, his shoes untied.

"Well, did you hit her?" asked the first boy.

"She had a little kid with her."

The second boy gave two slices of bread to the first boy. He had carried them inside his shirt. Then he handed back the stick.

*There was the time in Meuslowitz when Frank Bondy had shared with them the first bread they had in Germany. It was army issue, half rye flour, half sawdust. But then they thought they'd never eaten anything as good. That was when Frank had declared that he and Danny were his temporary helpers. They almost felt like pipls. Luckily Frank wasn't interested in pipls. They really were his assistants.*

*Danny was sure he saw one person in the bread line collect his ration twice. The person flushed, but Danny couldn't prove it. In the camp from which they came, people had strangled each other for a loaf of bread. But for this, when somebody went through the bread line twice, you could find many willing hands. Or it was arranged for the block leader to send him to the 'sauna', another expression for the ovens.*

*Justice must have really existed, once upon a time, but it had gotten lost somewhere, like a mote of dust that's trampled into the earth and then one day perhaps it's found again.*

*The person from the bread line, whom nobody listened to anymore, mumbled something about false accusations. To be someone's "assistant" in the camp was like a slice of bread–there were always two sides to it.*

"So you didn't hit her."

"Go ahead and eat."

"If you didn't kill her, she'll let them kill us."

111

"Yes," replied the second.

"You should have killed her, Manny."

The first boy raised the slice of bread to his mouth. The second watched him as he took a bite. His jaw tightened. He grimaced as though someone had run a grater across his tongue and palate and down into his throat.

He spat out the bread into the palm of his hand.

"What's the matter?" asked the second boy.

"I can't eat it."

"Why not?"

The first boy opened his mouth. It was full of blood. "It's too rough."

But it was fresh. The second boy stared at the slice of bread in his hand and cautiously bit off a piece. He spat it out immediately. The bread had also turned red with blood. He could feel the inside of his mouth swelling up.

"It's been a long time since we've eaten anything," the first boy said.

"She's got to give me some milk," the second boy replied.

"Get some for me too," added the first.

"This time I'll kill her if she doesn't."

"She could send half the village after us, Manny."

The second boy left without a word. The first opened his shoe. His whole heel had festered. He stared at it for a while, then poked around inside the shoe with a stick of wood. Afterwards, he leaned his head against the woodshed and closed his eyes. The German shepherd dog began to bark again, yet he felt a feverish quiet. The leg was swollen. The wound on his heel was full of dirt and pus. He didn't want to look at two clouds which seemed close enough to touch. He played with a few pebbles as if they were dominoes, shoving them back and forth, studying them closely. He wished everything that was still alive in his body and inside his mouth, would shrivel up and die. He grinned like a mad man. The clouds were like hummingbird eggs. He looked over at the chicken coop. But he didn't bother to get up and go in.

Then he looked through the open door to the shed, to that dark oblong in the light, to the dark aperture behind which he imagined there was some kind of peaceful animal. He couldn't see inside.

He stared at the pebbles and at the bread they couldn't even eat. He could just imagine Manny sticking out his tongue at the German woman to show her what had happened to the inside of his mouth. Then he'd hit her.

The first boy closed his eyes again. He couldn't understand what a woman with black hair was doing, living in a German village like this, while he and Manny, blond and blue-eyed, both of them (before their heads were shaved and the hair collected for mattress stuffing and for overalls for commandos from the German submarines) were considered as interlopers. He wondered whether the other villagers were all blond and blue-eyed, with nice straight noses, members of a race that gets purer, the farther north you go. Which meant the very purest of all are probably the polar bears. That's what his father used to say when he was feeling good and predicting that the Third Reich would collapse within five months.

The purest race are icebergs. The boy sat there, listening abstractedly to the frantic barking of a dog. He waited for Manny to come back from the farmhouse.

The woman watched them from the window. She could see them dropping the empty mugs into the bushes behind the woodshed when they'd finished off the warm, ersatz coffee she'd poured for them. She could see them cradling in their hands the potatoes she'd taken from the earthenware mixing bowl where she had intended to make dough.

She watched the smaller boy help the bigger one to get to his feet. He handed the heavy stick to his companion. The tall boy was between fifteen and sixteen, she guessed.

With the smaller boy leading the way, they trudged off toward the woods. The smaller boy had a cut on his forehead. He must have fallen on a rock or bumped into something. The taller limped.

She looked after them like a fish which inhabits the depths of silence. Her face mirrored the revulsion she felt but could not understand. It was obvious they hadn't had a thing to

113

eat for a long time. They were dirty and they stank. Along with the fear which, now that it was all over, had turned into curiosity and the comforting knowledge that nothing had really happened, the woman was amazed and bewildered that something like this could have happened on German soil. No foreigners ever come here.

There was something else . . . Red curtains were drawn back across the shutters. Seeing the curtain and the reflection of her face in the window, the woman was reminded of when she had been a young girl, before she married and had a baby. She picked up the child and watched the two boys as they made their way into the woods. It was like watching animals.

The sun shone in through the window, bringing the two boys into sharp perspective as they neared the edge of the forest. With one hand, she touched the buttons on her dress as if to make sure they were all fastened.

The smaller boy looked back at the farmhouse.

After she lost sight of them, she stood at the window as if puzzling what to do. But she'd already made up her mind. She put the little girl down and took her cape. Then she tied her kerchief under her chin, and her hand slipped down over her breast. Her lips were pressed tight, her eyes sharp and strict and her face was calm. The fear was gone, but an echo of anger was still there because she'd been so badly frightened. She went out and got the cups and rinsed them carefully. It was like some awful disease—she was repelled and fascinated at the same time. Inside, a satanic scheme vied with a tug to mercy. Had anybody seen them coming here? Were they Jews? Is that how Jews look? Like those boys? Even her dog had been afraid of them. She remembered all those things she'd heard over the radio.

"They're swine," she said to herself, and brushed her skirt. "Pigs!" she repeated.

The little girl's eyes were fixed on the lips of her mother.

—Wolves, the woman told herself. If that's how Jews look now ' the world's better off without them. No need to feel sorry for them if they go around scaring the wits

114

out of people. She had never seen real, live Jews before, though, so she couldn't be sure. But it was true that they bring decadence and chaos and all sorts of unpleasantness. They disturb the peace and quiet for which people work so hard. There was something about them that others could certainly do without. The boys merged into the misty forest.

She had the feeling that, in them, the war had finally come home to her.

Inside her bosom, there was something as dark as the fear she'd felt when she'd gotten married. Later, the child helped her overcome it.

She glanced over at the bed.

"I've behaved myself for too long," she said.

—They're nothing but tramps, the woman went on to herself. Who knows where they escaped from? Who knows how many people they've robbed and killed? They'll never change.

She touched her kerchief to make sure it was properly tied. Then she set out for the village. She walked toward the Mayor's office.

# 11

"I can walk better now," lied the first boy.

"We're going downhill," replied the second.

"This is hilly country, Manny."

"The main thing is, we're on our way again."

"Are you cold?"

From the top of the wooded hill, the whole countryside seemed to be sloping downhill. Judging from the terrain, they were in the border region.

"When somebody has so much that they don't even think about how much they used to have, they don't deserve to have it."

The first boy's foot was no help to him at all; it was just an appendage, like part of his trousers.

"I know I can make it now," he said.

*The second boy was recalling something that had hap-*

*pened on the train. They'd been on their way for three days*
*Another prisoner lay there, pale and bloodless and yellow*
*as a lemon.*

*It was painful to see how waxy he looked around the*
*nose and mouth and ears. When Kosta closed his eyes,*
*nobody knew whether he was still alive or not. Frank tried*
*to joke about it, saying Tom reminded him of an Egyptian*
*princess he had seen in a museum. "The only reason she*
*held together was because she'd been embalmed and stuck*
*inside a mummy case for 3,000 years, dressed in the finest*
*silks and wrapped with bands of satin as thin and tough*
*as the finest goat or calf skin. It's a wonder nobody stripped*
*her of her finery during those 3,000 years."*

*Kosta looked 3,000 years older than he really was. He*
*was skinnier than the day he was born. Frank knew he*
*was still alive; he could tell by the way his body shook*
*in rhythm with the train.*

*"By now, practically everybody's pretending he's almost*
*ready to kick the bucket," Frank observed.*

*But Kosta was really dying. He was dying slowly, wrapped*
*up in his blanket. The only reason nobody stole it from*
*him was because of lice. On the third day, he began to*
*smell, and a few people wondered whether they ought not*
*to shove his body out of the train during the night. The*
*guards would have been the last to object, except that they*
*were on German territory now and lice carry typhus. Kosta*
*had been lucky nobody wanted to touch his blanket.*

*When anybody wanted to relieve himself during the night,*
*they'd step on Kosta's chest or shoulders or even on his*
*head. That made it easier for them to pee over the side.*
*So Kosta stank of ammonia, too.*

*Tom Kosta had gotten a bad name among certain people*
*because in Theresienstadt, he'd complained to the Jewish*
*community authorities about "those rich, spoiled youngsters*
*who ought to be given something to do."*

*The train tossed Tom's skeletal body around, draped in*
*its rags and consumed by the biggest collection of fleas,*
*lice and assorted vermin ever seen on one person.*

*In the morning, Danny watched how everybody was*

*tramping over Tom. He made it clear that if anybody stepped on Kosta one more time in order to pee over the side, he'd catch hell from him.*

*It was a slow, lethargic dying. Danny practically had to kick him to bring him to in the morning. Then, like Jesus, he started picking the lice off Tom. He threw them over the side of the train. Danny had no objections to infecting all of southern Germany.*

*That was when Frank Bondy moved next to the Transylvanian guard, acting as though he was responsible for the other prisoners. Actually, it was just to get away from Kosta. "The sun will keep on rising and setting, boys," he told them. "It'll rain and the earth will dry out again. I doubt there have been many changes at the casino or in the clubrooms down in Monte Carlo. Aside from blackout curtains on the windows."*

*He used to talk about how "all symbols pale with time", that at that very moment, people were at the seashore and in the mountains, swimming and skiing, playing tennis and soccer, enjoying their hobbies, making babies—or not making them. Getting married and getting divorced. Women have their eyes on men and men are on the lookout for women. "And what does it prove?" he concluded.*

"Just imagine if we were girls," remarked the second boy suddenly.

"I'd rather not," murmured the first.

The second boy dragged Danny and his helpless leg through an anthill. The trees were getting sparser.

The first boy seemed to have lost all his strength except for what little it took to hobble along on one leg.

"Can you still make it?"

"Like my mother used to say, Manny—'if you want to live, you'll live. If you don't want to, you won't.' That's how nature's arranged it."

"We're going uphill again, Danny."

"A lot of it is just cowardice," the first boy whispered.

Both of them were off in their separate worlds that were

the same, but different too. Sunbeams skidded over the rocks.

Manny thought about why he hadn't killed that woman with the child. He was tired, so he thought about it slowly, and it was as though the thought brought with it something unexpected, something he hadn't counted on. It carried inside it many other things besides. There used to be a lot of mystery about killing, which wasn't really worth it. By now, all the mystery had been stripped away and it was naked, just as naked as they were.

Even in recollection, he got a bit of satisfaction with every German who got killed, as long as he and Danny were still living. Just like every German probably rejoiced over every Jewish woman, man or child who got killed. There was an edge of vengeance to it, done by someone else on his behalf, and gratification that it was possible at all, because it looked so impossible.

This is what it all boiled down to finally. There is a strange kind of strength in killing, even if you can recognize and control it. He knew the exact moment when he began to get tired of thinking about killing. He knew precisely when the change happened. And what this change might have meant if it happened while he'd been in the woman's kitchen.

It was like a rubber band which pulls you back towards it with the same strength as you pull in the other direction. It was not just ambiguous. It had many layers of meaning, like everything he'd ever encountered and puzzled over afterwards.

He couldn't explain it to himself yet, but he sensed what it does to a person when he can kill. It also had something to do with the fact that he doesn't. It had to do with himself, somewhere in the future, where he might perhaps ask himself a question—and be able to answer it.

To kill or not to kill has gotten into man like the blood his heart pumps out to the veins and arteries, or the air he inhales and exhales. Alongside the will to live, there was the multiplied determination to kill. It's always stronger than you are, but as long as you live, you can try to resist it.

Maybe he'd answer the same way now. And then answer something else. There are two kinds of people, the kind that are lucky and the others who aren't.

Once again, he thought about Frank who had somehow known that there's a difference between murdering someone and killing somebody because he wants to kill you or make a slave of you, as if you aren't even alive or simply vegetating in his shadow, for whatever reason—between killing somebody because you want something that belongs to him, because you despise him without even knowing who he is, and killing somebody because you hate him, because you know exactly what he's done to you and to other people. Because you were there and you've seen it happen. The difference probably gets blurred, but never entirely. It's never erased completely as long as you think about it, even if you're very tired and your thoughts are tired too.

He could have killed that Polish medic who amputated people's legs and hands and fingers when it wasn't necessary. He could have killed him even now because he hated him and he knew he had a right to feel that way. But even then, he'd been glad it had been somebody else who killed him. He knew lots of people (and the things they'd done) whom he could have killed without the least regret.

But he could remember situations when he'd thought it would almost be better to be killed himself than to kill.

It was different with that woman too because somewhere deep inside, he could still say to himself that he hadn't committed any of those great, important acts he shouldn't have. It was that old feeling he'd thought had been extinguished inside him. Like when Danny said the past was dead and non-existent for him, that you really might prefer to let yourself be killed, rather than killing somebody yourself.

He hadn't killed that woman because he would have felt guilty. The thing he was feeling right now was the same he'd felt while he was standing in her kitchen... the same instinct which told him things he didn't know or things he learned much later. Or never. There was a strange kind

121

of power which existed inside him, in addition to the real, predictable strength of his muscles, his legs and arms, and that he needed to keep his eyes open, that strange strength hidden away inside a man that he prefers not to draw upon, as if it isn't even there if you don't think about it. It had two sides to it too—the ability to strike someone down and kill him and the ability not to do it. A resistance to killing.

Some people are lucky and don't have to kill, even during wartime when killing is part of our daily bread, along with cold and hunger and lots of other things people don't otherwise do. Then there are the others who aren't so lucky and they get killed.

He thought about the child. Then, all of a sudden, it passed out of his mind. He forgot about it. He simply tried to overcome his tiredness. He knew in the marrow of his bones that now this was the most important thing in the world. Whenever he didn't overcome his tiredness—at least partially—he lost his sense of danger and that was both good and bad, but it could be the very worst. A sense of danger was always the first thing that saved him.

It had been a sense of danger which saved Danny and made him jump out of the train at the right moment. Then when the Transylvanian guard was shooting at them. And later when the American pilot had fired at them by mistake. But now Danny was so tired, he didn't even think of safety or danger. It was like when they were back there on the hillside. This sense is weightless, but you feel lighter without it, as though a heavy weight has fallen away.

As they walked on through the woods, he tried to put his weight on his foot so he wouldn't make it harder for Danny. But sometimes he forgot.

Danny trudged blindly along at his side. —As if he's dead, he added inwardly—. Maybe he's saving his strength for wherever it is we're going.

The first boy probably sensed that the other was worried about him.

"All I'm going to do is eat, Manny, once we get there," the first boy said softly. "I'm going to eat the whole, livelong

day. Then I'll loll around in a bathtub full of hot water
and eat and eat and eat some more."

He said it as though he knew it wasn't true anymore
either.

Birds sang in the treetops. It was a long, slow climb.
The second boy felt again that half-forgotten heat inside
him, the thing Bondy called the height of madness.

Exhaustion blotted out a lot of their initial fears. They
moved like sleepwalkers, clinging to each other so they
wouldn't get lost.

"Stop!" It was a rasping voice of an old man.

They both stiffened. Manny turned, but they still kept
moving. They didn't have the slightest intention of stopping.
Everything inside them had begun to function again. About
a dozen old men were moving toward them through the
trees, armed with shotguns.

"*Werewolves*," choked the first boy.

"They caught up with us," breathed the second. "Come
on!"

They both assessed the old men and could see that they
were a feeble handful of veterans who wouldn't have enough
wind to keep going much longer, just as the two of them
wouldn't either. But the old men were still fresh, while the
boys were tired.

The only thing to do was run away, to get across the
hill and disappear on the other side before the old men could
catch up with them. Shadows—or echoes—of Frank Bondy
melted into the forest. There was no time for him now.
The old man who had called to the boys, wore a civil defense
arm band.

A shot broke into the stillness of the forest. They ran
through the woods as fast as they could, but the faster they
tried to run, the slower they went.

"Come on!" hissed the second.

"I can't!" breathed the first boy.

The second didn't answer. He saw how the first boy was
gasping for breath.

"Come on!"

"It's impossible."

"Do you want to just drop dead?"

"I can't."

"You must."

More shots began to crack among the trees. They counted to twelve and the shooting began all over again. The men couldn't shoot in unison. It was hard work.

They swarmed forward, firing their rifles as they came. Some of them were wearing uniforms, or parts of them. The leader, with a hunter's cap and boar's bristle in the band, was the only one dressed like an officer, but with no insignia of rank.

"I can't make it," repeated the first as the second boy tried to drag him on.

"You can," gasped the second.

Bullets burrowed into the tree trunks and moss and earth and burst through some of the protruding roots.

The birds took fright and were silent. The best marksman was the leader, but even he wasn't much good. It was hard to get a good aim, going uphill.

One old man was pushing a bicycle. Some of them used their gun stocks like canes to help themselves along.

The old man in front stopped, took aim, then yelled at the boys to halt. When they didn't, he ordered the others to fire. The woods were filled again with the noise of gunshots.

"Come on!" urged the second boy, tugging at Danny's sleeve.

"Go on!" he breathed. "Run! I'll catch up with you in a minute."

The first boy pulled his arm away and the second took a few steps before he turned around. He refused to even think of surrendering to these old men. Danny lay on the ground, unable to take one more step, and the old men kept shooting. Their leader had run out of ammunition, so he borrowed a gun from another man.

"Leave me alone," groaned the first boy. "Leave me here."

The second boy was sure their only chance was to get to the top of the hill before the old men shot them. Or before they became infuriated at not being able to hit them. He didn't want to think about what would happen if Danny didn't make it, if they captured him alive.

"Don't be stupid," wheezed the first boy.

The second almost cursed. Then he grabbed the first boy and started dragging him up the hill. It was the heaviest thing he'd ever carried.

The first boy struggled to his feet. He still held on to his stick.

The second boy didn't want to think about how Danny must feel.

"Why don't you want to leave me here?" groaned Danny.

"I don't want to be alone," replied the second boy.

They came to a clump of bushes which lashed at their faces. They groped along, kicking up a pair of rabbits which disappeared into the underbrush. The boys' faces were scratched and blood-streaked.

"*Halt!*" yelled the first old man, reloading his gun. The magazine clicked. More single shots were fired.

The second boy couldn't catch his breath. Two German words rang in his ears, "*Halt!*" and "*Nieder!*" He felt a familiar lump scorching his chest and he waited for it to stab at his side.

The old men were crawling up the steepest part of the hill, moving a bit slower than the boys. They leaned against trees to shoot now, taking a longer time to aim. They advanced in a row, like trees with a few feet between them.

The first boy was almost unconscious. He let himself be dragged along, helping with his good leg as much as he could. Just when Manny lost his footing, the old man in front took careful aim. As the bullet left the muzzle of his gun, it whizzed through the trees and in the split second before it hit, several things happened all at once, only two of which were really important or perceptible. The bareheaded boy had been tugging the taller one in one direction, while the other was trying to break loose and duck into the underbrush. That was when Manny tripped over the

125

root. That was when the bullet which, a second before, would have shattered his spine, kept right on going. It merely ripped off a piece of his sleeve. It didn't even graze his flesh. It simply whistled out into a tuft of moss and pine needles.

The first boy, unsuccessfully, tried to get up. You could smell scorched cloth. The second boy grabbed Danny's collar and pulled him like an animal.

"Come on!" gasped Manny.

The first boy said nothing. "Let me be," he whispered after awhile. It was as if he were crying.

"Shut up!"

He dragged the taller boy as if he were a piece of his own body which had been torn loose. Maybe the reason why the first boy didn't speak, was because he was crying. The bushes and underbrush were the thickest in this part of the forest. They were so exhausted, they were ready to stop and lie down and die even before the old men reached them and shot them. The top of the hill lay just beyond a thin patch of green grass and they crawled the whole way on their hands and knees.

"Just a little farther," snuffled the smaller boy. "We're almost there, Danny." His whisper was scarcely audible. "Just a few more inches. Roll over, Danny. Roll over with me."

They had reached the top. They put their arms around each other and rolled until they were on the other side. The second boy retched. He didn't even turn his face or move away. He retched again.

Another volley of shots tore through the trees. Then everything was silent again and the birds began to sing.

The second boy wiped his mouth on a tuft of moss. By now, they were too tired to think that maybe the old men had been too scared to follow them over the hill. How were they to know whether the boys had guns or not?

"You should have killed her," the first boy said after awhile.

"It's all downhill now, Danny."

"She sent those bastards after us," the first boy went on. "Are you sick?"

"No."

"You're white as a sheet."

Wind stirred in the trees. Birds were singing. The trees waved and tossed as though they were going back to where they'd been before. The earth had a smell of early springtime. The woods sloped into a deep valley.

"How come you don't even notice when somebody wants to kill you, Manny? By now, I can tell," the first boy said.

They were tired and sleepy. They'd wanted to sleep so badly during the past three years—to sleep like they'd never slept before.

"It's great to be able to speak again," said the second boy.

He had a bitter taste of vomit in his mouth. He had nothing left in his stomach of what the woman had given them to eat. Looking at Danny, all he saw was a pair of rheumy, bloodshot eyes. "I feel like I'm all beat up," Manny said at last.

The first boy said nothing. Pain stabbed at his heel. A sharp stone, probably.

"If it had lasted a little longer, I'd have started feeling sorry for myself," the second boy went on. "When I was a kid, I went to kindergarten with a little German girl."

"If it'd been me that went into that farmhouse, I'd have killed her," said Danny. They trudged on for awhile in silence. "Are you still thinking about that little girl, Manny?" the first boy asked at last.

Suddenly, in the middle of the forest, they came to an asphalt highway. The woods, the moss, the sky, seemed like logs floating down a stream and the stream itself and everything around them was afloat, one layer of water on top of another. The boys sat down by the roadside and for several hours, they watched as a couple of trucks drove past in opposite directions. An army orderly roared by on a motorcycle. The noise of the motors did not seem as unreal as the sounds the forest and the wind made.

"This is the best place to wait, huh?"

"On a curve," the second boy said.

"Which way do we want to go? What do you think?"

"I'd say we ought to go downhill and to the right, Danny."

"I feel like my blood's run out. Like I'm all dried up."

They slid into a ditch by the roadside, crouched so nobody could see them from either side. An hour later, they heard the sound of a motor. It came slowly.

"Sounds like a truck, doesn't it, Danny?"

"Yeah, it's a truck," the first boy confirmed.

"Maybe we ought to get closer to the road."

"It's not going fast," the first boy said.

They lay down on their bellies. The truck was a small, three-ton model. The back was empty. The motor grumbled in the curves and the two boys decided this would probably be their best chance.

As the truck passed, the second boy dragged the first down the bank and made two running strides toward the truck. He caught hold of the side of the truck body. Danny was two hops behind. He had to put his weight on his bad foot.

The second boy held onto the side and pulled hard. Danny felt a stabbing pain in his foot as he tried to boost himself in, but his knee gave way and he fell. The second boy tugged his arm for a little longer and then he let go and jumped off the truck himself.

The first boy was lying on the highway with his stick beside him. Manny rushed back and began to shake him, telling him to get up, that they could still catch the truck. He shook him by the sleeve as if he was beating him. Or beating himself. Or the whole world. He didn't even look after the truck anymore.

It drove off slowly.

# 12

The room the boys were taken to, as prisoners, was across the hall from the mayor's office. It was in the same building as the village tavern.

They were told to strip naked and when it was discovered that they were not armed, they were allowed to get dressed again. Their clothes stank.

You could see into the tap room when the door was open.

—This must have been a school before they turned it into a tavern, Manny thought to himself. Tables and chairs were stacked in one corner.

They were the same old men who had hunted them down and shot at them in the woods. All they'd done was go around to where the highway cut through the forest. They had suddenly emerged out of the woods below the road and there they were, right in front of the boys, surrounding them, shotguns aimed. The mayor had a Luger. He warned them that if they made a false move, they'd be shot.

Then they had been brought here. An old man in a pre-war Czech army uniform, whispered something in German to the mayor. They had had to keep their hands up all the way from the road where they'd been captured, although Danny was allowed to keep his stick because without it, he wouldn't have been able to walk or even get up off the ground.

They were given permission to sit down on a bench. It was warm in the room.

—They'll probably have this bench scoured after we leave, Manny said to himself. They had stood for two hours with their hands up until finally Danny collapsed. Manny was alarmed by the red blotches on Danny's face. He was terribly thirsty and sorry he hadn't taken a drink from the puddle in the ditch along the roadside.

*When he shut his eyes, he could still see the hill he and Danny had crossed when they made their escape. But this time, all 2,000 prisoners were behind them and Frank Bondy was there too. He saw them clamber out over the sides of the freight car, as though jumping out of trains was some new contagious kind of Jewish disease. The women rebels from Warsaw jumped faster than anybody else.*

He was glad the vision didn't come back this time—watching all those 2,000 people sent straight from the train into the gas chamber.

*The American pilot had been circling the hill. He wasn't shooting anymore. He simply flew above the train like an aluminum star, wings tilted so they could get a good look at him. He took a few shots at the locomotive so they would realize his guns were loaded and that he had plenty of ammunition. He hit his target every time. Then he flew above the train, giving them plenty of time to get the message.*

*The hill was strewn with people. Like a teeming anthill. They lay sprawled across each other, tripping and stumbling onward as the black anthill moved slowly up the hill. The*

130

*guards stayed beside the train. Bracing themselves, they
shot the fugitives as though they were shooting rabbits.
Almost without bothering to aim. They hit a lot of their
targets. After a while, the hill was black with people who
were still running. They had to tread over bodies which
just lay there and bodies that still crawled or writhed.*

*Among those who were hit was Wanda, the pretty Polish
girl who had been dragged out of the sewer. She liked to
talk about mercy and humility and nobility. She had shown
Frank the scars on her breasts and thighs where she had
been bitten by trained German police dogs.*

*He saw Danny among them. And then there was some-
thing else. There was probably a lot the two boys never
told each other.*

*Maybe Danny had such hallucinations too. Maybe he
saw Manny going into the gas chamber.*

—The more tired I get, the more people I see going to
be gassed, he realized.

Finally, it wasn't just Jews and German invalids on whom
the Germans used their gas chambers. There were French
and English, Americans and Canadians and, of course, Russians and Poles. The whole world went into the gas chambers
in alphabetical order and everybody took his towel and soap
as if he really believed it. Manny blinked to shut out the
sight of it.

*Danny stopped to speak to the Polish girl as she lay on
the hillside. "You should have killed that woman," she told
him. "We would have killed her—and the child too."*

*Danny started running. Frank Bondy was beside the Po-
lish girl. She had been shot through the spine.*

*Frank dashed forward with two blankets, one under each
arm, and knelt beside her, rolling one blanket under her
head and the other under her spine. Wanda told him not
to lose time, that he should run. "—Not many people will
make it," she said.*

*Frank Bondy looked down at her and the wickedness faded
from his eyes. There was something else in its place. He*

131

*stayed with her. As he knelt there beside the Polish girl, bullets flew above his head. Wanda had had her share, even if she had been destined to survive. Frank Bondy tried to comfort her. He told her about Blanka, his fiancée in Prague, who would help to make her well again. Blanka had studied medicine for three and a half years before the Germans came and closed down the university. So she had some knowledge to build on.*

*Frank had a thousand and one faces. Some of them were quite likeable. But there were others that weren't. They were despicable.*

*The pilot circled over the anthill as it thickened and thinned, then suddenly he disappeared, taking with him the whistling sound his motor made.*

*The sky was empty again.*

Noisily, the old men came back from the tavern. They brought with them their mugs of beer from the keg that had just been tapped. The youngest among them set up a table and enough chairs so everybody could sit down.

They began to unpack the food they'd brought along. They kept their shotguns by their sides—old army guns, as old as the men themselves.

The men ate and drank and sang old German songs. Like the one about the little brother who liked to drink and leave his troubles at home. They sang another one about an imperturbable sailor, howling the refrain in unison: *"Keine Angst, keine Angst, Rosemarie..."*

After a few beers, they began to go back and forth to the toilet, buttoning their pants as they passed by the boys. There were no women in the tavern.

One man, who carried his gun over his shoulder like a game warden, began to dance. Somebody wound up an old victrola and they all sang along so the tavern rang with their merrymaking.

A white-bearded old man unwrapped a roast chicken from a piece of newspaper and offered some to anybody who was hungry. In a few moments it was torn to bits.

Then more old men started dancing. One of them was

dancing with his shotgun while he gnawed a chicken drumstick.

The boys were being guarded by an old man with a shiny Mannlicher on his lap. He cocked it, showing he was prepared to shoot if necessary. He wore a brown oilcloth coat that was supposed to look like leather. He was eating blood sausage, but he had no teeth, so he had to mush it up with his gums, along with chunks of bread. Laboriously, he pushed each mouthful out of its sausage casing and into his mouth. Then he carefully folded the paper in which the food had been wrapped.

—If there was water, the second boy thought to himself, I'd jump up and drink it out of that paper on his lap.

The first boy felt drowsy. His foot was throbbing. It was so hot in the room, that he dozed off. The pain soon woke him. It was as though his foot had taken on a life of its own.

"Danny... " the second boy murmured.

"No talking!" barked the old man immediately. Then he said it again: *"Nicht sprechen!"* His mouth was full.

The mayor called them in. The old man with the Mannlicher stood behind them. The mayor sat behind his desk in his belted leather coat. There was a framed picture of a young soldier on the wall. There was a black band across the corner of the picture.

Danny understood German better than Manny. He had just one answer when the mayor questioned them about where they came from, who they were, and what they were doing. He told the mayor they were from Dresden. Their papers had been burned during the February 19th air raids and they hadn't been able to get new ones from Prague yet. They'd walked because they didn't want to be a strain on the Reich's railroads.

"We haven't harmed anybody," put in the second boy.

He told the mayor he could phone the Prague police and check. They'd tell him that he and Danny had lived at Jungmann Square 4, across the street from the newspaper stand and the Italian ice-cream parlor. Unless there'd been some changes made in their absence.

133

They claimed they'd lost their papers and personal belongings in Dresden, where they'd been sent to work in a war plant.

"*Total einsatz,*" Manny volunteered.

The mayor didn't believe a word of it. At first, Manny had claimed he didn't know any German and now it gushed out of him like blood. The mayor made notes on a scratch pad, then finally he told them to take their clothes off.

"Every stitch," he ordered and snickered like a billygoat while they undressed.

He held his nose.

"All right, get dressed," he laughed knowingly. "On the double."

"We haven't done anything to anybody," the second boy insisted.

"We didn't have a permit, so we couldn't take a train," the first boy said.

"We don't even know where we are," put in the second.

"You're in Rottau," said the mayor.

"I'm not circumcised and they did it to Danny on account of an infection," said the second boy.

"It looks like they did it with a kitchen knife," said the mayor. "So that's how they maim you, hmm? So you have nowhere to hide. And then you go around maiming other people—here!" he pointed to his head. "And here!" he pointed to his pocket.

"We haven't maimed anybody," objected Manny.

"You've got just one minute to get your clothes on," said the mayor.

Danny's fingers were so clumsy, he had difficulty buttoning his pants.

"The motor patrol is coming for you at seven o'clock. They're going to take you to Karlsbad where you will be brought before a court marshal. They'll decide what to do with you," the mayor told them.

"Get moving," ordered the old man with the Mannlicher.

The boys sat down on the bench again.

"We'll grab the sentry, Danny . . . "

"Humph," replied the first boy.

134

"Don't forget to hang on to your stick!"

"*Ruhe!*" bawled the old man.

"Sit on the right hand side so you can jump out, Danny."

"I told you to keep quiet!" the old man repeated.

"I have something I want to tell the mayor," spoke up Manny.

"There's no use," the old man told him.

"They did it to Danny because of an infection. That's what I want to tell him."

So *Karlsbad*–Karlovy Vary—was that near! We must have been wandering around in circles. This was all Czech territory: Karlovy Vary—*Karlsbad, Rottau*—Rotava. *Home*, as Frank used to say, is a country where you're at home without having to take anybody else's home away from him.

*Frank understood German better than they did. He knew Spanish too, and English and Portuguese and Yiddish. His French was as good as if he'd been born in Monte Carlo. Yet with all those advantages, he'd stayed behind in the train that was supposed to be going to Dachau.*

*Frank had said, "There's no sense keeping count of those who do knuckle under. There are too many."*

—We didn't knuckle under, Danny and I, the second boy told himself. The worse the circumstances, the less is forgiven.

The mayor went on about how, even though the war was almost over, they must not and would not be allowed to rule this country.

—The mayor feels at home here too, he thought.

The mayor had a snout like a cucumber and a leathery face. He told them they mustn't be surprised if they'd be shot, considering that they had viciously attacked a German peasant woman and stolen bread, potatoes, milk and coffee from her, not to mention all the other things they probably had on their consciences. On top of that, they hadn't obeyed orders to halt given by a German civil defense unit. Did

135

they suppose they could fool them by taking several hours to walk a few hundred meters through the woods?

It was almost seven o'clock. There were anti-tank traps along the road, which had probably delayed the patrol.

The second boy looked down at Danny's feet. Those used to be his shoes. Before that, they'd belonged to Leonard. Danny smelled. He held his cap in his hands. The muscles and angles of his face had gone slack and his shoulders sagged. It was a slackness the second boy had seen before and it frightened him.

—If I had Frank's watch now, I might sell it to one of those guys, Manny thought. A clock hung on the wall beside the old man, its brass pendulum swinging back and forth. It struck the half hours with a mellow, hollow tone.

*Before his eyes, the second boy could see a door with a brass name plate. The plate was bare. He placed his finger on the doorbell and pushed it. This was the place he always came back to, fearful that nobody would be there.*

"Danny," he whispered.

"There's no point to it," the first boy replied at last.

The sun was sinking. The clock struck seven. It had a gala sound, as though it was summing up everything that had ever been and ever would be. The second boy listened to the clock strike and he knew it would go on ticking for many years to come. Seven o'clock would pass and eight o'clock and in between, the clock would chime to mark their passing. The clock had a mild tone. The bench they were sitting on was polished smooth as glass by thousands of backsides of farmers who would go forth at daybreak tomorrow to plough and sow and hunt and shoot and milk the cows, trying to make a paltry living and have a little fun. They'll say their prayers and have babies and fertilize the fields, building houses and killing game. The clock would go on telling time and striking the hours and half hours—a hundred times, a thousand times—until the works break down and somebody buys another clock.

136

The pendulum swung back and forth. The sky darkened slowly. It was one of those lovely, fragrant evenings of early spring, layered with meaning. The darkness wrapped around it like some delicate fabric.

*Now he was remembering the German hospital in Theresienstadt where he and Danny and Frank Bondy had worked, digging trenches for the anti-aircraft shelters.*

*At noon, Frank brought over a jug of soup from the ghetto. It was thin slop, but it was better than nothing, since they were only fed once every twenty four hours and it was hard work.*

*He had been standing in line one time when Frank was dishing out the soup. He had pushed in front of somebody else and Frank gently motioned him to the end of the line. Frank's hands were elegant and immaculately clean in those days. With a kindly smile he went on ladling out the soup conscientiously, taking his time so everybody got a fair share from the bottom.*

*At last, there were only the two of them in front of the vat. Frank poured a ladle full of soup into Manny's canteen. When he stepped back, Frank touched his elbow with his elegant, clean hand. Because of his upbringing, experience and principles, there were probably very few germs on Frank's hands. Then he quickly gave Manny another helping of soup, as brimming as the first.*

*Something had broken. The beautiful confidence in how things would be someday–because there were still people in the world who thought it was important–had silently crumbled, falling apart like a house of cards.*

*Nobody knew. Frank should have been proud of himself and pleased. Nobody had even noticed that second helping. Frank peered into the kettle to see how much he had left.*

*The construction of a pure, just, human being, convinced that the way things are right now is simply a temporary phenomenon, was poured out with that second ladleful of soup, with Manny's second helping.*

*Frank smiled paternally, as if to say, "don't play dumb." And he sent him away.*

137

*It was as though he was bragging that if you were even
slightly clever, you could save more than anybody could
imagine from the servings you give to twelve ditch diggers.
Everything evaporated, turning itself into muck and filth
which was choking the world and from which you could
never escape, as long as you lived. He stank of that filthy
world himself.*

The mayor came out of his office. He passed them by
without a glance. Danny was asleep. He looked as if he
was already dead. But he hadn't died. Now and then, his
body twitched and his legs would jerk, like a dead fish.
The mayor said something to the older men in the tavern.
They laughed and then, for some reason, they applauded.

"*Herr Bürgermeister* wants to talk to me," announced
the old man with the Mannlicher.

The second boy nudged the first.

"We'll grab the guard, right?"

"Sure."

"Swear you will, Danny?"

"I swear," he promised in a flat voice.

The second boy was thinking that maybe if they'd look
sufficiently miserable, the guards might not tie their hands.
The clock struck the half hour. —This must be that same
beautiful feeling that comes over you when you're going
to die, Manny decided. Danny was ready to die right now,
he told himself.

He could hear the mayor talking, "Take them out in front
of the building at seven sharp," he was saying.

"*Zum Befehl, Herr Bürgermeister,*" said the man in the
old officer's uniform.

"You know what to do."

"*Jawohl, Herr Bürgermeister.*"

# 13

Now it flashed through the second boy's mind that no patrol was coming, that the old men were going to finish the job by themselves. Briefly, he could see an image of the two of them lying on the road in their rags, between the woods and the tavern. They'd been shot.

The old men also looked like crippled, helpless birds. But at the same time, in comparison with the two boys they still had some strength left, despite their feebleness. But it was a good thing they didn't beat or kick or mistreat the boys in all the ways they knew only too well. But they'll shoot them. They will probably shoot them together. They're still capable of shooting them at the same time. If it had to be, it'd be a good thing if it would happen fast, at least, and at the same time.

*That evening in Meuslowitz when the Germans had started shooting people and everyone else had to watch, Frank Bondy said that there was nothing new in what was happening. He whispered as though he was going back to the pyramids, to some ancient canals full of sand, as though the camps were one with the pyramids and those canals, their bottoms covered with the muck of flesh and blood of people who no longer lived, and who were yet to come; as if the killings were simply part of a single current—what was, what is, and what is yet to be.*

A woman walked through the hall into the tavern. She had blond hair, blue eyes and a pale skin. She wore a black kerchief over her head.

She reminded Manny of the woman who had given them the bread, the woman they didn't kill. Danny stared at his ailing foot.

The woman was wearing a leather coat like the mayor's. She was probably his wife.

She attracted him in the same sort of way that Frank Bondy had been attracted by the Polish girl who had been gang-raped. That lovely thing that's only found in women.

*In his mind's eye, he could see the double bunks in Theresienstadt, and he remembered the first time he had gone there with a girl. It had formerly been stables, what the Germans called Jägerkaserne. Men brought girls there with bellies big as leeches.*

*The girl he went with later did anything men wanted but she wouldn't allow them to go inside her. That was because she was scared of getting pregnant. She made an exception with him, though, and later with Zdenek Pick and little Milan Oppenheimer. Actually, it had been his father who pushed him into it. He kept asking a little too often whether he'd ever had a woman for himself.*

*Maybe Father had known that something like this was going to happen, that the clock would strike and the order would be given to take them out in front of the building, just as the sun was setting.*

*Maybe he had an idea that when the clock finished striking, the signal would be given for the German rifles to be cocked, ready to fire.*

*The clear chime of the clock reminded him of the best things in his life. Or else the things he'd wanted to do someday. The things Father had known.*

*The girl had been kind. She put her hand between his legs and caressed him so sweetly that he forgot his embarrassment and apprehension that he'd be incapable. She led him on, the way you lead a child into a forest which it's been frightened of at first, but later comes to enjoy.*

*He wasn't the first boy who had been with her that afternoon and he noticed how moist she was to start with.*

*"It has a sweet taste," she told him. "It smells like fresh-cut grass in the evening." She went on: "You're like a young horse. You'll have luck with girls."*

*Nevertheless, the boy who came out from behind the curtain was different from the one who had gone in. He didn't remember everything that had happened. He didn't even wait for Pick and Oppenheimer. There were a lot worse things you could get in exchange for an ounce of margarine.*

*Right afterwards, the whole world felt like one big moist, juicy, furry woman.*

*When he left her, he went into the toilets where everybody else went when they wanted to weep. Then, later that night, he did it by himself and it was almost better than the first time.*

*The stars had shone brightly that night. He was just as alone as everybody else is on this planet earth out in the middle of the universe and even if they aren't alone, they feel as if they are.*

*Next day, he'd met his own father walking down the main street of the ghetto with that same girl and another man. Dad introduced him as her husband.*

After a while, the woman came out of the tavern. She had the calm expression of someone who had had plenty of sleep.

Her eyes reminded him of two brown almonds.

—I've seen eyes like that before, Manny thought to himself. Leonard had that kind of eyes. So did Zdenek Pick. And little Milan Oppenheimer. And Frank Bondy had eyes like that.

And then he realized that they weren't eyes at all—they were the crows that had followed them through the forest. He was almost glad they wouldn't have to go back to the woods anymore, even though it had been a refuge. He could feel the woman's eyes on him and he almost expected them to peck his own eyes out.

—There was somebody else who had eyes like that. My God, Mother! For a second, everything went black. He couldn't move. Not even his little finger. He'd never felt so helpless in his life. Then he opened his eyes and moved one finger.

That was when the clock began to strike the hour of seven—six deep-throated clangs and then the seventh, which would tip the balance of their lives toward the other side.

The mayor stepped out on the porch in front of his office. The woman moved next to him. His face looked as though it had been molded out of an old leather belt.

"Stand up!" said the man in the old officer's uniform and the hunter's hat with the bristle.

The second boy helped the first to his feet.

"Take off your clothes. Just leave your shoes. Fold your things and take them under your arms."

When they were naked, the taller boy in his shoes and the smaller with his feet wrapped in rags, they just stood there. Danny held onto his stick and the second boy's arm was around his neck.

"Take them out in front," the mayor told the old man.

*"Gehen sie,"* ordered the old man.

The mayor and his wife stared at the two naked boys. Outside, the sun was setting. It grew dark slowly. Another wave rushed in on Manny, and Danny was in it, too. He knew he'd stick it out this time. He was glad he was with Danny.

The woman looked at their bodies as though she were searching for something she couldn't find.

142

Both of them paused when they got to the front of the building. The second boy gripped the first boy's arm more tightly so he wouldn't trip and fall.

—We've said all there is to say by now, Manny decided. Maybe Danny will be the first, because he can't walk by himself. Danny couldn't even stand alone.

The rest of the old men stood in front of the building in a horseshoe formation, their rifles lowered.

"Take them into the woods," said the mayor. The woman was smiling slightly.

"Prepare to fire," commanded the old man.

There was the familiar clicking and clatter as the guns were cocked.

Manny limped forward, keeping one arm around Danny's shoulder. But by now he was so tired, it was all the same to him. He clutched their clothes under his other arm. He waited quite calmly to find out which one of them would be shot first. He didn't look around. Danny didn't either.

—This is where it ought to happen, the second boy thought to himself. One last order. Then those cracking noises. We'll only hear the first ones.

"It's good," he said. "This way, it's good."

Manny could feel the earth under his feet, the moss and rocks and stones. He gazed off into the woods, and he saw Danny out of the corner of his eye. He was waiting to hear the crack, multiplied by as many as there were old men. That noise would have everything inside it that had ever happened—the forest, their footsteps, other sounds. Tension, which was drowned by tiredness, was almost like walking half asleep.

Nobody would be able to follow them from now on. Beyond the shadows of the forest where it was already night, morning would come only with the sun. They did not look back, but stared straight ahead, above the treetops. They were alone.

"Danny . . . " whispered the second boy.

The first boy raised his eyes and looked at him.

"Everything's all right," he whispered. That was the last thing he said.

143

Still nothing happened. The second boy had no idea what time it was. He had no more visions of things that had happened to him before. Nothing. All that was left was the thought of what might happen—where would those two bullets go? And then what would not be here anymore?

They were about twenty steps away from the building now. The second boy pressed the first boy closer. Danny squeezed Manny's shoulder too. Both boys were bareheaded. A wave of resignation passed between them and a shared realization of where they were going, of the awesomeness of what they were walking into.

They were two small, naked bodies in shoes and rags, one tall, one smaller, hanging on tightly to one another.

But they still heard nothing.

It only came later, when the stars were shining high above their heads, after they had disappeared into the darkness, under the trees at the edge of the forest. They pushed deeper into the tangle of low branches and it was as though it had begun all over again and it would always end the way it was ending now—once, twice, a hundred times. As often as they tried. In the moldy smell among the roots and bushes and stones and moss and pine needles and even if they'd have turned around, the mayor's brick house and the tavern wouldn't be there anymore. That was where the path stopped, where the woods grew dense again.

They faded into the night, like a slim double shadow. The stillness was not silenced.